To Mom

Madness Heart Press
2006 Idlewilde Run Dr.
Austin, Texas 78744

This is a work of fiction. Names, characters, places, and incidents either are the product of the author's imagination or are used fictitiously. Any resemblance to actual persons, living or dead, events, or locales is entirely coincidental.

Copyright © 2010 Wrath James White
Cover by Luke Spooner

Second Edition
isbn: 978-1-955745-55-0
www.madnessheart.press

EVERYONE DIES FAMOUS IN A SMALL TOWN

INSPIRED BY TRUE EVENTS

WRATH JAMES WHITE

A Madness Heart Press Publication

CHAPTER 1

It was July 4th, and the air smelled of fresh cut grass, burning charcoal, and charred beef and pork. It was the aroma Mika had come to associate with summer. Hank Williams Jr. sang about all his rowdy friends on a stereo system with one speaker that Mika's parents had owned since the seventies. It still had an 8-track along with the cassette and the record player, and her dad even had the little plastic inserts used to play the old 45 singles. Mika wasn't even sure you could buy vinyl anymore, let alone 8-track tapes or cassettes. But a CD player or an iPod wasn't in the budget. Her father was saving up for a new fishing boat.

Storm clouds rolled in over the mountains, and

the air smelled damp and moist. The weatherman had insisted that the clouds would pass and there wouldn't be any rain for another four days. Her father had believed him despite his own eyes. He fired up the grill bright and early. Rain be damned.

Joe Shaw, her father, was cooking pork ribs, beef brisket, hamburgers, and hot dogs on the barbecue, and he had added wet hickory chips to the charcoal. It created a thick, delicious smoke that billowed across the lawn and made her eyes water along with her mouth. He had a Coors beer in one hand and a pair of tongs in the other, constantly flipping, poking, and prodding the meat. Every once in a while, he would drop the tongs and pick up something that looked like a long-handled paint brush and slather more barbecue sauce on the ribs and brisket. The smells made Mika's stomach growl.

Every adult who passed, including her mother, had a beer or a cigarette in their hands, and most had both. Once in a while, she would ask her father for a sip of his beer, and depending on his mood, she'd either get a long swig, a sip, or a slap. Today, Joe had been in a good mood, and Mika was feeling lightheaded. It was a good feeling that she always enjoyed. The alcohol had almost given her the courage to ask for her own beer. Almost. She knew better than to ask. It was one thing to ask for a sip of Joe's beer but quite another to ask for her own can.

She was only sixteen, and a girl. Her brother, Cliff, was two years younger at just 14 years old, but he could already reach into the cooler and grab his own beer without anyone saying much of anything. They would laugh and think it was cute when he got drunk. He was a boy. If she asked for a beer or showed signs of being more than just a little tipsy, she would get slapped around. Girls weren't supposed to get drunk. So she had learned to sit down when she started feeling lightheaded, before she staggered or fell, in an attempt to keep the grin off her face no matter how funny everything appeared after a few Coors. Mika weighed eighty-nine pounds, so it didn't take her much to get drunk after the painkillers she'd taken that morning. Her friend Jenny had given her a couple Dilaudid to help her come down after she'd been up all night on meth. They weren't mixing well with the alcohol.

Mika knew she was pretty. Everyone told her as much. She had long black hair, *Indian hair*, light brown almond-shaped eyes, full lips, and a nose that was wider than she would have liked but which did nothing to detract from her beauty. Her father called it a nigger nose, but she didn't care. It was her mother's nose, and he had thought her mother pretty enough to marry. Mika was so thin she was almost bony. Still, her father was constantly telling her to watch what she ate. He would point to her mother and tell her how thin her mother had been when they met.

"Now look at her," he would say, but then he would pat her mother on the rump or wink at her and tell her she was still beautiful.

But Mika saw the wounded look on her mother's face. She knew her mom was hurt even though she would have never said it. Instead, her mother would smile and look away or busy herself cleaning. Their house was as clean as an intensive care unit, and her mom popped enough Xanax to keep Mika's entire high school stoned. Xanax and Vicodin were as popular among the housewives in this town as meth and weed were among the teenagers.

Mika didn't like to clean. It was easier just to watch what she ate, and if she ate too much, she would promptly excuse herself, go into the restroom, and stick a finger down her throat to bring it all back up.

Mika didn't look anything like her father, and she knew that was one of the reasons he was so mean to her. He suspected Mika's mother had been unfaithful and that Mika wasn't really his child. He was right. Her mother had taken her to meet her real dad, a tall Indian man from the Owens Valley Paiute Reservation who was on the tribal council. Add that to the fact her dad had never wanted a girl and had wanted two boys.

Maybe that was why he hadn't lifted a finger when a big Indian girl from the reservation beat her up last month and stole her lunch money. She'd had to go without lunch, and her dad had told her to fight back next time. Mika suspected her questionable paternity was the reason her dad hadn't called the police last year when her Uncle Jeff, his brother, had raped her. He had beaten him up, and Jeff wasn't welcome in their home anymore, but he still had no criminal record and didn't have to register as a sex offender, which meant he could abuse some other little girl somewhere whose parents had no idea the kind of monster they were allowing to come around their kids. But Mika wasn't allowed to bring that up anymore. As far as her dad was concerned, he had handled it.

She shook her head and tried to chase the memory of out of her mind: the stench of beer, cigarettes, and sweat that still made her nauseous whenever she smelled or tasted it. She thought instead about the barbecued ribs and brisket she was about to eat along with her mother's potato salad, green bean casserole, deviled eggs, and sweet sun tea. Mika smiled and felt herself begin to lean too far to the left, almost falling out of her lawn chair. She caught herself, quickly wiped the smile off her face, and sat up straight in her chair. The beer and Dilaudid were starting to get to her. She looked over at her dad, only to find him staring back at her suspiciously.

"Have you been stealing beer from that cooler again?"

"No. All I had was what you gave me." She smiled again despite herself, and this time, a giggle slipped out. Joe dropped the tongs and charged across the lawn faster than his short, stubby, hairy legs seemed capable of carrying him. Mika watched him draw back his hand as if she was watching in slow motion.

"Are you saying I made you drunk? You lying little bitch!"

She wasn't sure what slapped her first, his

words or the back of his hand. The impact spun her head sharply and knocked her face-first out of the chair and onto the grass. When she looked up, her father was walking back to the grill. She turned her face to the sky just as the first raindrops fell. Her head felt cloudy and heavy, as if all the blood had rushed to it. The sky above her was turning slowly, as if she was on a merry-go-round. Mika wasn't sure if it was the beer or the slap or if the world was really spinning that fast.

"Shit!" her father yelled as droplets of rain sizzled on the grill.

Her dad began removing the meat from the barbecue while her mom and her brother gathered up the lawn furniture, the tablecloths, paper plates, Tupperware, and plastic utensils. Mika took this moment to slip away. No one would notice she was gone. They hardly noticed when she was around unless she was doing something they didn't approve of.

The rain began to fall harder, pelleting the earth with little high-velocity projectiles of water that stung Mika's skin as she walked to the road, headed toward the Owens River. She loved the way the river turned savage during a rainstorm, becoming rapids with white-capped waves. She liked to sit and watch it pound the riverbanks and splash up onto the grass.

The left side of Mika's face was still red and swollen from where her father had slapped her. Her bottom lip had swelled up like a gumdrop on one side. The cold rain mixed with Mika's warm tears and ran down her face. Cars passed her as she shuffled down the dirt road, splashing through puddles of mud. Every vehicle that passed contained a familiar face. Many of them waved at her, and some beeped their horn or shouted her name from their open windows as they passed. Mika kept her eyes forward and down, watching her pink Converse All-Stars soak up rainwater and collect an ever-thickening coating of mud on their soles as she made her way toward the river.

All Mika had ever wanted was to make her father proud of her the way he was of her brother, Cliff. Cliff could do no wrong in the eyes of Joseph Shaw. Her dad went to every one of her brother's little league games and even attended the practices. He used to spend hours in the backyard working with Cliff on his swing and his fastball. In the two years that she had played, her father never attended even one of Mika's soccer games, even though she was the star player on her team. When she had finally quit soccer and signed up for softball, he came to her first two games but stopped coming after it became apparent she had no aptitude for the game.

As Mika wandered along the road, she began sobbing harder as she recalled the last softball game her father had come to see. She had hit the ball for the first time after several tries at bat. The ball had gone sailing deep into left field, and Mika had run as fast as she could. She made it to first base just as the outfielder retrieved the ball. Mika kept going. She was almost to second base when the outfielder threw the ball to the second baseman. Mika slid. She dove at second and slid just like she had seen the pros on TV do. When the second baseman tagged her with the ball, her hand was already on the base. She was safe. But she had skinned both knees and forearms. Blood ran down her arms and shins. It hurt so badly that Mika began to cry.

The coach called timeout and ran over to check on her. Mika looked around for her father, expecting him to come and comfort her, clean her wounds, and cover them with band-aids. When she finally spotted her father, heading across the field toward her, there was nothing comforting in the look on his face. His face was red, and the veins were standing out on his neck and forehead. She knew the look. It was the look he got when she had done something wrong and had embarrassed him. The look he got just before he slapped her or yelled at her and called her a dumbass. Mika tried her best to stop crying before he knelt down beside her, next to the coach. He held a Coors Light in his hand and took one last swig before kneeling down and taking a look at her bleeding arms.

"What the hell are you crying for? You're holding up the whole game. If you can't play without crying like a little baby, then you shouldn't play at all."

"It's okay. She just skinned her knees," the coach said, wiping the blood from her legs and forearms with a cold wet towel.

Her father ignored him.

"Stop crying! Do you want me to take you out of the game?"

Mika shook her head and sucked up her tears. Her father stood up, took another swig of his beer, and walked back off across the field. That was the last game he had ever come to. Mika had finished the season, hoping at each game to see her father in the stands but dreading it as well. He had never come, and when the season ended, so had her sports ambitions.

The river was as wild as Mika had thought it would be. A tree along the river bank had fallen over into the water, its roots clinging stubbornly to shore as the rushing waters tried to drag it away. The river was the color of liquid mud and was filled with leaves, twigs, and branches, along with the occasional potato chip bags, soda and beer cans, newspapers, paper plates and cups, and other refuse tossed in by unscrupulous campers and picnickers.

Mika sat by the edge of the river and watched the trash rush by. Watching the water had always helped clear her head. She thought about nothing—not her neglectful father or her spoiled brother, not even her uncle and what he'd done to her. She just watched the water.

Then she heard the laughter.

It sounded like children's laughter. High-pitched giggling, coming from the water.

Are there kids playing in the water? Mika wondered.

There was no way little kids could have swam in that current; it was much too strong, and they would have been swept away.

But then she heard it again, coming from further

downstream. Mika stood and ran along the river bank in the direction of the giggling. She couldn't see anything. She stopped after she'd run a couple hundred yards. She should have found the kids by now. They couldn't have been that far away. But the sound had stopped. Mika was about to walk upstream when she heard a new sound. Crying. She strained to hear over the rain and the rushing water, but there it was. The sound of children crying. She looked around. The sound seemed to be coming from where she was standing. She looked down into the churning waters. She couldn't see anything.

She crept closer to the edge of the water, and then she saw a little pale hand reaching out of the roiling brown stew.

"Oh shit! Oh god!"

Mika reached out for the child's hand, but it went under. Then she saw others: more hands, feet, and heads bobbing in and out of the water. There appeared to be maybe a dozen children, all drowning in the river. Their dimpled faces were twisted into expressions of terror. A chill raised along Mika's spine. She shivered and backed away. Something wasn't right. They were all crying but not screaming, not yelling for help, just weeping.

Even when their eyes met hers, they didn't call out to her, they just continued to weep. And something else wasn't right. All the babies looked the same.

They were white. Pale, sickly white, with dark eyes and dark hair. All the same age. Toddlers. A river full of toddlers no more than one or two years old, sobbing as they drowned.

Mika backed further away, and their sobs grew louder, more insistent, as if she was hurting them, somehow causing them to suffer through her inaction. But there was no way she could save them all, even if she tried. She might drown herself. And she was scared. Not just of the river but of the children. They weren't right. The way they reached out to her was wrong. The way they stared at her, the way they cried, and the way they all looked the same. It was all wrong. They were all staring at her now with their cold black eyes full of tears. Their pale, chubby little arms reached for her, imploring her to help. Mika shook her head and took another step backwards.

Then they smiled and began to laugh, all of them, laughing as they sank beneath the waves. Mika turned and ran.

She ran all the way home in the rain, slipping and stumbling and falling down more than once.

She kept running until she reached her front porch. She wrenched open the front door and slammed it behind her. Her shoes were caked with mud, and rainwater streamed from her clothes and hair, forming a large puddle on the floor. She hoped her father had passed out by now. He would lose his mind if he saw the puddle of mud on the floor, if her mother didn't get to her first.

Mika took a minute to bring her breathing back to normal and stop the trembling in her legs, then walked over to the hall closet to get the mop. The mud puddle and her muddy footprints were almost gone when her mother walked into the living room. Mika could tell that her mother wanted to get angry, but it was too late now. The deed had already been done and tidily undone.

"You do know how to make a mess, don't you? Make sure you take off those shoes before you go to your room. I don't want you tracking mud all through the house."

Sometimes Mika wished her mother would get drunk too, or smoke weed or something. The woman was pulled tighter than plastic wrap. Mika took her time mopping up the rest of the muddy rainwater, enjoying her mother's obsessive-compulsive discomfort. She knew that it was killing the woman not to grab a rag and jump down there on her hands and knees to add her own elbow grease to the restoration of the vinyl floor to its former scuffed and scratched lackluster beauty. Any minute now, she would snatch the mop out of Mika's hands to finish the job herself. That would have been fine with Mika, except her mom would complain the entire time about having to clean up after her, just loud enough to bring Joe storming into the room to see what all the fuss was about. And that would end in more bruises for Mika. She quickly mopped up the rest of the water just as her mother neared her breaking point.

She pulled off her sneakers and left them on the front porch. Then she walked to her bedroom, pausing to hug and kiss her mother goodnight.

Her room was the typical post-pubescent shrine to pop culture. Atypical only for the bizarre mix of music styles. Posters of Marilyn Manson and Nickelback competed with those of Kenny Chesney, Toby Keith, and Billy Currington, as well as Ludacris and Little Wayne in an incongruous collision of Rock, Country, and Rap. She knew she was the very definition of white trash. Old issues of *Seventeen* and *Cosmopolitan* magazines sat on a chest at the foot of her bed. The walls were painted pink—baseboards, door handles, and all. Mika had painted it herself one weekend in a fit of creativity. Scarves hung from a mirror plastered with photographs of her and her friends. An old TV sat on a milk crate diagonal to her bed.

Mika lay down on her bed and fished a small Ziploc bag out from between the mattress and box spring. The bag was no larger than her thumb and contained a small, powdery pinkish-white stone. Mika shook the stone out into her hand and opened the drawer in the nightstand by her bed and fished out a razor blade from among the knickknacks inside. She picked up one of her magazines and began shaving chunks off the white rock with the razor and then chopping them up into a fine powder.

Methamphetamines were a white trash high. That's how Mika thought of it, anyway. Coke was expensive. Heroine was a death wish. But meth was even cheaper than crack. The Indian boys cooked it up right there on the rez. She could buy it with the money she stole from her mother's purse. Mika didn't care. She was proud to be a redneck. And to her, that meant riding horses, smoking Marlboros and unfiltered hand-rolled cigarettes, drinking Keystone and Mikey's, and snorting meth.

She separated the powder into three thin lines, then took a ballpoint pen from her nightstand and removed the ink reservoir. She slid the hollow pen into her left nostril, pressed her index finger against her right nostril, lowered her head to the magazine, and snorted the first line. Her nostril burned. Her eyes blurred with tears. A foul taste filled her mouth like she'd swallowed a mothball. Her nose began to run, and her nostrils went numb. She closed her eyes, rubbed her nose repeatedly, and waited for the rush. Her heart began to beat faster. She could feel it pounding in her chest. She knelt down and snorted the other two lines. Her exhaustion fled, and she felt like she had enough energy to run a marathon.

She switched on the old 17″ black and white TV and turned to channel 11. They were talking about Michael Jackson's death on TMZ. Mika couldn't have named more than two Michael Jackson songs if she had a gun to her head. That was all way before her time. Mika found a hairstyle she liked in *Cosmopolitan*. It was long on one side, short on the other, and shaved in the back. She took a pair of scissors from the bureau and began to cut her hair.

As she hacked away at her hair with the scissors, she recalled what she had seen in the river earlier.

She hadn't been high then. She had been a bit tipsy but not really drunk. Of course, she hadn't been taking her Haldol. It made her feel dizzy, and worse, she gained weight when she was on it. She preferred to self-medicate. But meth wasn't exactly an antipsychotic. It didn't do shit to keep the voices away or the monstrous shadows, the raging angry ghosts she saw in her peripheral vision. All it did was stop her from caring about them.

Sometimes Mika had full hallucinations where she would find herself talking to her friends when she knew they were home in their beds. Once, she'd spent half the night talking to Big Nate only to find out the next day he had been in the hospital in a coma for two days after being kicked by a mule he'd been trying to shoe. It had freaked her out, but not enough to make her go back on her meds.

It was easy for her to dismiss the water babies as just another symptom of her schizophrenia. But something about them had seemed so familiar. It was as if she had seen them before. Mika shuddered as she remembered their cold black eyes and their bloodless white skin. Those mirthless smiles. And then their cries. Weeping but not screaming, not crying out for help as they drowned in the river. Just sobbing as they floated amongst the waves.

Cold chills slithered across her skin, and Mika imagined that it was tiny wet hands. Children's hands. She began to scratch, trying to scratch the feel of their tiny fingers from her skin. She scratched long rivulets in her flesh, the skin peeling back and revealing the pink muscle tissue beneath. Mika watched trails of crimson roll down her arms, down the back of her hands, and off her fingertips onto the floor. On the television, an old fat man in a business suit was yelling loudly about government run healthcare. He was red in the face, and veins were bulging in his neck, but Mika couldn't understand exactly what it was he disagreed with. As she watched the blood begin to clot on her scratches, she thought maybe free healthcare would be a good idea.

Mika turned off the TV and turned on the little alarm clock/radio on her nightstand. She tuned it to the local station and resumed cutting her hair into a ragged, uneven mess. Carrie Underwood was singing about Jesus driving a car or something, then the song ended and Mika heard the radio broadcaster announce that a teenaged boy had drowned in the Owens River. They were withholding the kid's name and photo until his family had been notified. Mika didn't need to see a photo to be certain it was someone she knew. She knew everyone in this town.

CHAPTER 2

"What the fuck did you do to your hair?" Jenny asked. Jenny was Mika's best friend and sometime drug dealer, though Jenny usually shared whatever she had or gave it away for free. The problem was that she rarely had meth. Jenny preferred coke and weed.

"I cut it."

Mika's hair was all but gone. What had been long black locks was now just a patchy tightly cropped crew cut that looked like it had been cut with a chainsaw.

"Oh, shit. What did your mom and dad say?"

"They haven't seen it yet. My mom's probably gonna freak. My dad won't give a fuck. He'll say some shit about me lookin' like a dyke or something and go back to drinkin'. He should be happy. He never wanted a girl anyway."

"Are you a dyke?"

"Fuck you! I wouldn't fuck you if I was."

Jenny laughed, but there was something forced and artificial about it.

"You sure? I suck a good dick. I might lick pussy good too."

Jenny reached out and tickled Mika, who swatted her hands away.

"Get away from me! You're sick!"

They both laughed.

"Something is seriously wrong with you."

"Ain't nuthin' wrong with me, girl. I just like to fuck."

Mika shook her head.

"You need help."

"Oh shit, did you hear what happened to Howard last night? Can you believe that shit?"

"Howard Redhawk?"

"He drowned last night." Jenny seemed almost excited by the news. It was something unusual, something out of their normal monotonous routine of drugs, sex, alcohol, and ennui.

Mika and Jenny sat at the gazebo in Bishop City Park, smoking weed and drinking wine. It was the early afternoon, but with no school for the summer, there was nowhere they needed to be and nothing to do.

The gazebo was a brown wooden structure in the corner of the park. From there, they could watch the traffic on Main Street and try to spy a familiar face among the passing vehicles. Traffic was slow today. Everyone was either at work or still sleeping off the previous night's drinking.

Mika scowled at her friend even as she took the rolled joint from her hand and raised it to her lips. She inhaled deeply and held it in until she began to cough, then she passed it back to Jenny, shaking her head from side to side as marijuana smoke billowed from her open mouth.

They had both grown up with Howard. Mika had dated him for a few weeks last summer. He was the first guy she'd ever slept with willingly. They had fucked every day, at his house, under the bleachers at school, in the woods in back of the church, in the woods by the bridge on Winuba Lane, in his Mustang. Their relationship ended after she threw up in his car when she'd given him head and he'd cum in her mouth. She'd tried to swallow and her stomach had revolted, spewing half-digested tacos and Strawberry Hill onto his lap and the floor of his car. She had been so embarrassed she'd never gone out with him again and had barely spoken to him since.

Now he was dead, and Jenny was beaming, excited to have something to gossip about. Mika wondered why she hung out with the girl.

Jenny was a year older than Mika. She was the town whore, a rich bitch who liked to slum with the natives and the white trash, using her money to literally buy friends. When Jenny was around, there was always plenty of alcohol and drugs. That was the only reason people tolerated her. That and the fact that she was easy and had big tits. Guys would come hang out with them, drink themselves stupid, and end the night grunting and moaning between her fat, sweaty thighs in the back of a truck or in the sagebrush while Mika tried her best to ignore them.

Jenny's parents had money. They bred prize horses. But you wouldn't know it to look at her. She wore designer clothes but not Prada or Chanel. She wore Baby Phat and Echo Red, dressing like she was in a hip-hop video. She usually wore her hair in cornrows and wore a diamond earring in her nose. Like Mika, Jenny's musical tastes ran from Country to Heavy Metal to Rap. She was a little overweight but liked to flaunt her large ass, constantly talking about how Black boys would go crazy for it even though there were no Black boys in Bishop. There was only one Black family in the entire town, and they had a daughter.

Mika knew that the only reason anyone bothered fucking her was because they could. She was no challenge, and most of the guys in town had such low self-esteem they would rather risk an STD with a sure thing than risk rejection trying to talk to girls who were less promiscuous. Just hanging out with her had begun to ruin Mika's reputation. Not that she was exactly a nun. She liked to fuck as much as anybody. She just liked to think of herself as more discriminating. Still, Mika really liked Jenny. She was her oldest friend in the world, even if she was the town whore.

"I heard it on the news last night. They didn't give a name, though. They just said some kid drowned. I can't believe it was Howard. How did it happen? Did anyone see it?"

"He was drunk. He just took off his shirt and jumped in the river. Drowned his fool self."

"In the middle of the rain storm?"

"He must have been fuuucked up! You know how them Indian boys get with some firewater in them."

"Howard wasn't like that. He didn't get drunk like that. I mean, he drank, but nothing serious. He wasn't a drunk."

Jenny took another hit off the joint, then tilted up a bottle of Boons Farm and took a long drink. Mika rolled her eyes. Jenny smiled at her and shrugged.

"I guess. He was a FAS baby, though. You know they have low tolerances."

"FAS?"

"Fetal Alcohol Syndrome. His mom drank like a fish when she was pregnant with him. It didn't take much to get him drunk. He had alcohol in his blood. He was probably drunk as fuck."

Mika shook her head and turned away. She couldn't understand how Jenny could be so callous about the whole thing.

"I dated Howard once, you know." Mika tried her best to hold her tears back. She had never loved the gangly, awkward farm boy, but he had been her first, not including her perverted uncle.

Jenny took another swig and drained the bottle. She turned and smiled crookedly. Her eyes were slow and unfocused.

"Maybe it was a suicide."

"A suicide? No. Howard wouldn't kill himself!" Mika scowled at Jenny in disgust.

Jenny just shrugged again.

"Why would he take off his shirt and jump in the water in the middle of a thunderstorm then? Maybe he saw the water babies or something."

Mika turned and stared at Jenny with her eyes wide.

"What did you say?" She grabbed Jenny by the shoulders.

"Chill, girl! What are you getting so excited about? Why you trippin'?"

"What the fuck did you just say about water babies?"

"It's just an old Indian myth."

"Tell me about it."

"It's just a myth."

"What are they?"

"They say there are these spirits that live in the water, demons or ghosts or something. They look like little babies. You hear them crying sometimes at night. Sometimes you can see them. They look like they're drowning or something. But if you go down to the river and try to save them, they pull you under and drown you. Sometimes they can look like other people, dead friends or relatives calling you from the other side."

Mika sat there staring at Jenny with her eyes wide and her mouth open.

"You okay?" Jenny asked.

"I saw them. I saw them last night."

"What? Really?"

"I was walking down by the river during the storm, and I heard them. At first, it sounded like little kids laughing and giggling, like on a playground, but then they started crying. I went to the river thinking it was some kids playing in the water and that maybe they had gotten hurt. The water was really rough because of the rain. But when I saw them, I knew there was something wrong. They all looked alike. They all had black hair, black eyes, and this sickly looking pale white skin. Like they had been in that water a long, long time. They were calling out for me to help them, but I got freaked out and ran."

"Whoa. That's wild. How do you know they weren't real kids? They could have really been drowning."

Mika was looking straight ahead. Her eyes had glazed over as she remembered the way the babies had looked bobbing around in the muddy water, crying without screaming.

"Nuh uh. These weren't normal kids. What would a bunch of toddlers and infants be doing floating down the river in the middle of a thunderstorm? And if a dozen babies drowned, don't you think that would have made the news? I mean, Howard makes the news but a bunch of babies drown and nothing? Even if somebody managed to rescue them all, it would have been all over the news."

Jenny took another hit off the joint, nodding in agreement.

"Yeah, you right. So you think that's what happened to Howard?"

"I don't know. It makes sense."

"Demon babies drowning Howard in the river makes sense?"

"I mean, it's crazy, but it would explain a lot."

Jenny looked down at her feet and then up at the sky, then over her shoulder, trying to avoid Mika's eyes.

"Um uh … I hate to ask this, but … um … were you high? You know, when you saw them? Were you fucked up?"

"Not until after. I ran home and tooted up right after I saw them. I had to get fucked up after that. I mean, I had taken that Dilaudid you gave me, like, a couple hours before, and I drank a little beer, but all that did was make me sleepy. I was fine by the time I walked all the way to the river."

"Were you on your meds?"

There it was, all out in the open now. Mika wished she had never told Jenny about her condition. Now Jenny would think the water babies were just another one of her hallucinations.

She frowned and fought to keep the tears from her eyes. She hated talking about the shadows. Why couldn't she be normal?

"I don't need them anymore. I'm okay." Now it was Mika's turn to avoid eye contact.

"Uh huh."

Jenny did not look convinced.

"You know, you should dye it."

"What?"

"Your hair. You should dye it pink or something. Then people will think you've gone punk rock. 'Cause right now it just looks like you fucked up your hair."

"Fuck you, Jenny."

CHAPTER 3

Dark clouds roiled across the heavens, hiding the moon and stars from sight, threatening to burst. As Mika walked toward the bridge, she was in total darkness. The streetlamps were out. Except for the occasional porch light or the infrequent headlights from a passing car, the veil of night was absolute and impenetrable. Mika walked blind up Winuba Lane.

There was a bonfire down by the stream made of burning tires, and a thick, noxious smoke billowed into the air, smelling of tar and chemicals. Mika wondered if they were all going to wind up with emphysema from inhaling that crap every weekend.

This end of Winuba Lane was on reservation land, so they never had to worry about cops coming down there to fuck with them. It was out of their jurisdiction, which made it a perfect place to get high. That night, it looked like every teenager in town was up at the bridge huddled around the makeshift bonfire, inhaling the burning rubber into their lungs even as they drank themselves into oblivion and smoked whatever was available. The smell of marijuana lingered just beneath the smell of the flaming tires.

Tonight, everyone was talking about Howard's death. Many of them had tears in their eyes. The rest just looked drunk or high.

Teddy was there. He was already drunk, and his eyes were bloodshot from crying. He threw a bottle at the bridge, and it shattered at Mika's feet just as she was walking across to where everyone was gathered. Mika was about to cuss him out when he staggered away and began punching a nearby tree. Teddy had been Howard's best friend. He was obviously not taking his buddy's death well.

Teddy was tall and thin with a square jaw and thick black hair that came down to his neck. He looked more like a Cherokee than a Paiute, like the Indians you saw on TV. He was a forward on the high school basketball team. Mika always thought he was handsome, though he was a bit of a jerk. He'd once laughed at her when she'd gotten drunk and shit her pants. He'd started calling her Shitty Butt Cheeks. Seeing him cry in public was uncharacteristic, disconcerting. It made him far more human than she ever considered him to be or ever wanted to know he was.

In Bishop High, Teddy was like a god. He was the high scorer on the basketball team, the one who always pulled out that last-second game-winning shot. The one who fucked the head of the cheerleading squad under the bleachers, then fucked the homecoming queen in her daddy's car the very next weekend and bragged about it the next day in school. He was the bad boy your dad would never approve of but secretly wished he was. He was who girls like her dreamt about when they masturbated. Mika was too young to see her idols fall. She had a lifetime ahead of her in which to be disillusioned.

"He was my bro. You know? We was like … like brothers, ya know? Why would he do that? Why would he just kill himself like that? It had to be an accident, right? It had to be, right?"

Teddy was looking for someone to commiserate with. He was walking in and out of the crowd of drunken and anesthetized teens, weaving and staggering, drooling beer down his T-shirt as he attempted to drink and talk at the same time, looking for someone to make sense of his pain. Mika had always had a crush on Teddy. Seeing him in such obvious pain, so vulnerable and needy, made her predatory instincts rise to the fore, though a drunken quickie with a guy sobbing in his beer and struggling to get it up wasn't really her idea of a good time.

Mika hugged her friend Jenny as she reached the bridge. She could feel as many eyes on her as were on Teddy. She must have looked like shit with her hair hacked to pieces. Jenny was wearing a skirt so short that half of her enormous ass was sticking out. She was the only white girl on the bridge besides Mika, but Mika had always been welcome there because everyone seemed to know that she was half Paiute even before Mika herself knew. She couldn't help but be amazed at how her mother had managed to keep it a secret from her dad.

Mika grabbed a Keystone Light from a twelve pack nearby. She quickly gulped it down and reached for another. She had catching up to do.

"Why does everyone have to be staring at me

and shit?"

"You should have worn a hat. You look like a little boy with a bad haircut."

"Fuck you, Jenny."

"I'm just sayin', as a friend. You look rugged. You should have worn a hat. You need to lay off that meth. That shit be havin' you do some crazy shit. Especially that cheap pink shit that's goin' around. Tracy Meadows picked out all her eyelashes last week on that shit. She looks even sillier than you do."

Mika shrugged and took another sip of her beer. "It's the only thing that keeps me sane."

"When have you ever been sane?"

"Not funny, Jenny. Fuck you very, very much."

Mika turned her back on her friend and stared off into the darkness. She stared down at the stream, and for a moment, she thought she saw a tiny pale white face glaring at her out of the gloom. When Jenny wrapped her arms around her and kissed her on the cheek, she almost screamed.

"I didn't mean it like that. I was just fuckin' around. I'm sorry."

"It's cool. Whatever." Mika continued to stare out at the stream. Every so often, she thought she saw the face again, drifting along on the current.

She even thought she could hear a child's high-pitched giggle amid the sound of the trickling stream and the crackle of the bonfire flames. With all the drunken laughter around her, she couldn't be certain it wasn't just one of her schoolmates chuckling over a vulgar joke. But it didn't sound right. The lilting bird-like titter didn't come from behind her but from beyond her, out there, in the blackness beneath the bridge.

Mika shivered despite the July heat and rubbed the goosebumps on her arms. She turned and watched Teddy again. He was leaning against a tree, drinking a bottle of Keystone and staring into the water trickling beneath the bridge. He was looking at the exact spot Mika had been looking, right where she thought she'd seen the baby's face. The expression on his face was one of confusion. He was squinting and trying to peer deeper into the dark. Mika was just about to walk over to him to ask him what he'd seen when Betty Stone, a girl from Mika's class, wandered over to him and offered him something on the back of her hand that Teddy knelt down and snorted.

"He's trippin' tonight. I can't believe that rugged bitch is givin' him coke. She's just hopin' he'll get fucked up enough to fuck her skinny ass."

Jenny hated any girl who was getting laid other than her, especially if they had better drugs than her.

"He probably needs it. He looked pretty tore up over Howard."

"I've got some 'shrooms. I should give him some of those."

Mika shook her head and took another drink of her beer. "Uh uh. Trust me, he don't need to be seein' shit right now. That wouldn't be a good idea. What if he has a bad trip? He's pretty fucked up already."

"It ain't LSD. This is natural. It'll be cool."

"Don't, Jenny. I'm serious. It's not cool."

"It'll be cool. Don't worry."

Jenny walked over to Teddy while Mika watched, still taking sips off her beer. Mika shook her head as she watched Jenny feed Teddy a handful of mushrooms. Mika had already watched him snort a line of coke and drink Lord knew how many beers, not to mention whatever he'd taken before she'd shown up. Mushrooms were the last thing he needed. It occurred to her how fucked up her friends were that they gave their condolences in the form of narcotics. Their solution to a friend's grief was to get him high.

Mika saw someone staring at her in her peripheral vision and turned to see Tonya Bowhunter point at her hair and giggle. Tonya was full-blooded Paiute and almost twice Mika's size. She was not the type of girl Mika would have wanted to get into a fight with, but Mika wasn't in the mood to be fucked with either. She held up her middle finger to the girl, then pulled the hood of her sweatshirt up over her head to cover her hair and turned her back, hoping the girl wouldn't run up behind her and punch her in the head. At least she didn't have any hair for the girl to pull.

"I see him! I see him! He's alive! Howard is alive! He's right there under the bridge!"

Teddy was freaking out. Several boys from the reservation struggled to restrain him as he cried out and tried to get to the bridge. Mika ran over to help. As Teddy roared and raged in their grasp, reeking of alcohol and sorrow, Mika clasped her hands on either side of his face and looked him in the eyes.

"Teddy! Teddy! It's not Howard! That isn't Howard down there! I've seen them too. I've seen them too, Teddy. It's not him."

Teddy stopped struggling. He relaxed in the embrace of his friends. Mika hugged him, and everyone else released him. There was a crowd around them now, and Mika felt awkward hugging the coolest kid in school while he was in the middle of a nervous breakdown. She expected him to start crying, to scream, or push her away, but instead he just stood there, not hugging her back but just slumped limply against her, allowing himself to be hugged.

He sighed deeply, then stood up to his full height and looked down at Mika. He smiled, and Mika felt butterflies take flight in her intestines. He turned away from her and reached out for one of his friends from the basketball team, who caught him as Teddy staggered forward. He propped him up, one arm wrapped around Teddy and one of Teddy's arms draped across his shoulders. His name was Johnny somebody. He was a big Paiute from the rez who played on both the basketball and football teams.

"I just want to go home," Teddy whispered, and they began to walk back toward the bridge. A white owl flew over the road, and Teddy and Johnny both stopped abruptly. They stood there for a moment at the entrance to the bridge as if uncertain whether or not to cross it. Teddy turned around and smiled at Mika one last time before continuing up the road.

The smile was heartbreaking. It looked like the valiant false courage of a condemned man walking toward the gallows, filled with fear and sadness. In that sorrowful expression, Mika sensed a desperate unspoken plea, as if Teddy was begging her to save him. But save him from what? Mika didn't know and wasn't sure what help she could have been even if she had known. She was too messed up to be anyone's savior.

After Teddy left, the gathering by the side of the bridge began to thin; everyone wandered off in different directions, disappearing into the night as if slipping behind a huge black stage curtain. Soon, it was just Mika and Jenny.

"I told you not to give him those 'shrooms."

"It wasn't the 'shrooms. They don't work that fast. He had just eaten them when he started trippin'. I don't even think he had finished chewing them all."

"Well, something freaked him out."

"It wasn't anything I gave him. But who knows how much shit he was high on? He was just swallowing or sniffing whatever anyone gave him. It was like he was tryin' to kill himself."

"He said he saw something under the bridge. I

thought I saw something down there too. I heard giggling coming from down by the stream. I thought I saw a baby's face down there. Then I saw Teddy staring at the exact same spot right before he freaked out."

"The water babies again?"

"I thought it was … you know … because I haven't taken my medication, but Teddy saw them too."

"He said he saw Howard down there, not some white babies with black eyes."

"I don't know, maybe we should go down there and take a look. If we're together, we can keep each other safe."

Jenny shook her head vigorously as she turned away from Mika and lit up what was left of her joint, now little more than a roach. She inhaled deeply and coughed out a small cloud of marijuana smoke.

"Uh uh. I ain't goin' down there. What if there's some pervert down there? What if that's what you and Teddy saw? Some freak down there watching us and beatin' off under the bridge? Besides, water babies are supposed to try to drown you. How they gonna drown somebody in that little-ass stream?"

"You can drown in six inches of bathwater,"

Mika replied.

"I'd be surprised if that little-ass stream was even that deep in most places."

"Come on, Jenny, you gotta help me. I need to see what's down there. Just to make sure I'm not going crazy. You don't know what it's like, never knowing what's real and what isn't. Not knowing if you're just hearing things or if someone really spoke to you. Not knowing if that cute guy you see across the street is really there or just in your head."

Jenny stared at Mika through eyes clouded with beer and narcotics.

"Fuck. Is that what it's like? That's fucked up. I mean, you really can't tell when you're hallucinating?" Jenny asked.

"Sometimes I can and sometimes I can't. They all seem real. I mean, when it's something really weird, I can usually tell it's fake. But weird shit happens in this town. Remember the time Lonnie got drunk and cut his nipple off and ate it? I thought that was a hallucination, but then I found it really happened."

Jenny laughed. Even her laughter sounded slurred.

"Yeah. That was fucked up. He just has this

little dimple looking scar there now where his nipple used to be."

"I don't even want to know how you know that."

Jenny smiled. "'Cuz I fucked him."

"I told you I didn't want to know."

"He's got the biggest cock I've ever seen," Jenny replied.

"Ewww. He's got the biggest moles I've ever seen."

"You're just jealous."

"Are you gonna help me or not? Just come down real quick, and we'll take a peek?"

Jenny looked down at her feet, stomping in place in aggravation. She tried to light the roach again and burnt her fingers. She tossed it to the ground and shoved her hands into her front pockets.

"Can't we just come back in the morning?"

"Whatever I saw down there might be gone by then."

"And that's bad why?"

"Come on, Jenny!"

"Fuck! Okaaay! I really hope that this is just one of your hallucinations."

Actually, Mika hoped it was as well. She didn't

know what she would do if Jenny saw them too. Then what? Were they supposed to go to the police and tell them that little demon babies who live in the river killed Howard? Or were they supposed to do nothing and just live with what they knew until the next kid died?

They held hands as they wandered down toward the bridge, where the darkness was magnified a hundredfold; not even the light from the moon and stars reflecting off the water penetrated the crypt-like gloom.

"Shit. Can't we just get high and make out like we did when we were kids? There's nobody around. I bet I could make you cum."

Mika stopped and stared at her friend for a moment. Clouds had covered the moon, and it was now so dark she could barely make out her girlfriend's face. For a moment, Mika had the eerie feeling that Jenny's face was gone. She was afraid that when the moon returned, she would find herself staring at the soulless black eyes and bloodless corpse-like pale skin of one of the water babies. Jenny's hand felt cold and clammy despite the heat and humidity, further convincing Mika that she was holding the hand of some lifeless thing that had crawled out of the water.

Mika closed her eyes and shivered, stifling a scream. She wanted to let go of her friend's cool, moist hand but was afraid that if she did, Jenny would lose what little nerve she had left and turn around and go home. Mika swallowed hard and rubbed the goosebumps on her arm down with her free hand. She then squeezed Jenny's hand firmly and kept walking.

"What's up with you and this lesbian shit lately? You ain't gettin' enough dick?"

"I don't know. Maybe I'm bi?"

"Maybe you'll just fuck anyone and anything," Mika answered.

Jenny laughed. "Yeah. Maybe that too."

"Let's just take a peek. I swear, it'll be quick."

They continued walking until they were standing beneath the bridge.

"Hello, little muffin."

Mika screamed.

CHAPTER 4

Uncle Jeff looked exactly the way he had the last time Mika had seen him, right after her dad had kicked his ass. His left eye was a huge purple and black hematoma that had completely swollen shut and was weeping sluggish tears out of the corner. The left side of his mouth was also swollen and cut, and his teeth were stained red with dried blood. Her father obviously favored his right hand when he was beating the shit out of someone. Maybe she hadn't given her father enough credit. He had done a job on Uncle Jeff.

His nose was busted and tilted crooked on his face, with blood leaking out of it down into his moustache, which was caked with dried blood and snot. He wiped repeatedly at the blood with the back of his hand as he spoke. Uncle Jeff reached a hand out of the water, pawing at the air, grasping for Mika.

"Come here, little muffin. I won't hurt ya. I just want to make you feel good."

He was naked as he rose from the water. Water dripped from his shoulder-length mullet down his hairy back. Somehow, he had been standing in the water up to his chest even though Mika knew that the stream was no more than a foot deep. He had a fat stomach, skinny arms, and a flabby chest that hung down like sagging breasts covered in matted black hair.

"Get the fuck away from me, you fucking pervert!"

"What? What's going on?" Jenny asked. Mika still held her hand as she cried out in anger at the apparition of her uncle.

Jenny squinted into the darkness beneath the bridge, trying to see whatever Mika had seen while backing away from it at the same time, dragging her screaming friend away with her.

"Oh, come on. You know you liked it. You had the tightest little pussy I ever had. You know you want some more of this." He groped at his dick, which was fully erect. His penis was small and unimpressive, just the way she remembered it. A short, thick, stubby little uncircumcised cock that had been inside of her, that she'd had in her mouth. She retched and regurgitated onto the rocks and weeds at the edge of the stream, emptying her stomach of all the beer she'd consumed that evening. As if sensing her thoughts, her uncle began stroking himself as he leered at her.

"Why don't you come suck it for me just like I showed you? Come on, you know how I like it, little muffin." Uncle Jeff smiled. His bloody teeth looked almost black.

Mika turned and ran up the embankment, back toward the road.

"Don't run away, little muffin. Get back here, you ungrateful little cunt! If I can't have you, I'll take Cliff. I'll bet he's even tighter than you are."

Mika stopped running and whirled around to face the grinning, wet pedophile standing in the water behind her. But he was gone. The stream was empty. Where her Uncle Jeff had stood threatening her was now just empty night. Where his loathsome voice had filled the air was now just the trickling of the stream.

"What happened back there? Who did you see?" Jenny asked, terrified and out of breath, still dragging Mika away from the bridge.

Mika snatched her hand away from Jenny and continued staring down at the stream.

"You didn't see him?"

"I didn't see anybody. I just heard you start screaming and then yelling about some pervert you saw down there."

Mika turned to look at Jenny. "But you didn't see him standing there naked? You didn't hear the things he was saying to me?"

Jenny shook her head. The moon returned in time to illuminate the expression on the girl's face as it changed. Mika recognized the expression immediately. It was one she had seen many times since she'd first been diagnosed with schizophrenia. It was that "Oh my God. She's out of her fucking mind," look. That combination of fear, confusion, and pity. She hated that expression and hated it even more on the face of her best friend.

"I'm not fucking crazy. He was there. I saw him!"

"Okay. Okay. He's gone now, though, right?"

Mika looked back down beneath the bridge. The night was once again a solid impenetrable wall. "Yeah. He's gone."

"Then let's get back to the fire."

Mika looked past Jenny at the ring of burning tires in the clearing at the edge of the woods and shook her head. "Everybody's gone. I'm going home."

"We can't just hang out a little bit? I was serious about making out. I've never really been with a girl before. I want you to be my first."

Mika ignored her.

"Do you have anything to bring me down?" she asked. "I've been doing so much meth I haven't slept for three days."

"Three days? That's probably why you're hallucinating. You can't be doin' that shit. It ain't healthy. You've got to sleep."

"What do you have?"

"I've got some Percocet I took from my mom. That'll probably put you out."

Jenny reached into her pocket and handed Mika a small ball of aluminum foil with six small pills in it.

"Thanks. I'll see you tomorrow."

"Hey, Mika?"

"Yeah?"

"What … what did you see down there?"

Mika sighed and turned away, shaking her head, trying to decide whether to answer. When she turned back, her eyes were hard and cold. "Remember when I told you what my uncle did to me?"

Jenny nodded.

"I saw him down there, my Uncle Jeff, the fuckin' rapist pedophile."

Jenny put a hand over her mouth, and her eyes turned soft and moist. "Oh shit. I'm sorry. That's creepy as fuck."

"Yeah."

"Do you, you know, see him a lot? I mean, do you dream about him and stuff? Do you have hallucinations about him?"

"Never. Not before tonight."

There was a long silence while they both tried to decide what to say next. Both of their stares gradually drifted back toward the stream. The normally soothing sounds of the water running over the rocks now sounded ominous somehow, like the drip of blood from a fresh wound.

Jenny was the first to break the silence. "Hey, don't tell anybody about, you know, me trying to get in your pants."

Mika laughed. "Stop trippin'. It ain't like you tried to rape me or somethin'. You asked and I declined. No big deal. You wish I'd tell people. It would probably make you the most popular girl in school."

"Really?" Jenny lit up.

"Trust me. You don't want that kind of popularity. You've already got enough of those kinds of friends."

"Lesbians?"

"No, stupid. People who just want you for what they can take from you. Sex, alcohol, drugs. You need real friends."

Jenny nodded. "Like you?"

Mika smiled. "Like me."

The two girls hugged. When Jenny kissed her, Mika didn't resist. Even when Jenny's tongue wriggled its way into her mouth, she didn't push her away. She even found herself returning the kiss. They held each other for a long time, lips locked together, tongues intertwined, and Mika had to admit, it wasn't bad. Jenny was a damn good kisser. When they broke off their embrace, they were both panting heavily. Jenny reached out for her again, but Mika held up a hand to ward her off.

"Good night, Jenny."

Jenny smiled and nodded again, dropping her eyes bashfully. "Okay. Good night, Mika."

Mika walked quickly back up to the road and began the long walk home.

56

CHAPTER 5

Johnny drove slowly down Pa Ha Lane. He passed block after block of squat single story reservation houses with their brown wood siding and chain link fences, unkempt lawns bursting with weeds. Some of the houses had neatly manicured lawns, their owners not yet given in to despair, still taking pride in their homes. Some even had gardens filled with fruits, vegetables, and small rows of corn. These were few and far between. They passed mobile homes on blocks. Feral mongrels, reservation dogs, darted in and out of the darkness between the moonlight, fleeting shadows hunting rats and possum and foraging through garbage.

Right up until he'd passed out, Teddy had been raving to Johnny about seeing Howard under the bridge. Then he'd begun screaming about white owls and white buffalo he thought he saw along the roadside. At one point, he'd been convinced that they were being pursued by a pack of wolves as they drove around the reservation. He kept yelling for Johnny to drive faster. He almost had Johnny convinced that they were being chased. It was so dark even with his high beams on that Godzilla could have been following them and Johnny didn't think he'd be able to see him through the dense shroud of night and the thick trees that lined the road on either side. Johnny kept swiveling his head, trying to see what Teddy was seeing—until Teddy insisted he'd seen the wolves stand upright like men, running nearly fast enough to catch up to the truck. That's when Johnny had nearly lost his patience with the whole thing. Johnny didn't believe in werewolves or skinwalkers or any of the old Paiute myths. He was a modern man. He believed in science and reason and drug induced paranoia and delirium.

When Teddy started screaming about snakes in the car and tried to crawl over Johnny to open the driver's side door and jump out, Johnny had almost driven the car into a ditch. He had to swerve to keep the vehicle on the road. That's when Johnny hit him. He bawled up a fist and cracked Teddy right on the jaw, knocking him unconscious, which wasn't hard considering how drunk the kid was. Johnny wasn't sure why his friend hadn't passed out on his own long before then but figured it was the coke he'd snorted that had been keeping him up.

Teddy was snoring now. Johnny couldn't help but stare at him. He knew what the girls at school saw in his friend. Johnny wasn't gay, but he wasn't stupid either. Anyone could see that Teddy was handsome. He had a square jaw with high cheekbones and bow-shaped, almost girlish lips. And he was tall with a lean, hard, muscular body. He looked like Hollywood's idea of a noble Indian warrior. But Johnny could kick Teddy's ass any day of the week.

There was no one in the entire school who could take Johnny in a fair fight. He was the better hunter too, though hunting wasn't something Paiutes were known for. But it wasn't like he was out there chasing down buffalo with a bow and arrow and a spear. He hunted deer and quail with his Winchester 94 and always bagged more than Teddy, who'd missed every deer he'd ever shot at. Johnny even got better grades than Teddy in school. Teddy was damn near an idiot whose only hope for getting into college was athletics.

In the old days, Johnny's skills would have been far more valuable to the tribe than Teddy's. Johnny would have been a big man among the other Paiutes. But not now. Now, the fact that Teddy looked like a movie star and could dunk a basketball and shoot a three-pointer made him a hero amongst the tribe, especially the teenage girls. Johnny had to admit that he resented his friend more than a little bit for it. But Johnny knew that in twenty years when he was a successful businessman and Teddy was falling off a barstool somewhere, boring everyone within earshot with tales of his former fame as a high school basketball star, it would be Teddy who would envy him.

The truck slowed and came to a stop in front of Teddy's cookie cutter house on Barlow Lane that looked exactly like every other house on the street, like government housing, which is pretty much what it was. "Reservation" was just a fancy word for "projects" as far as Johnny was concerned, and he wanted to escape "the Rez" as badly as low-income Blacks and Latinos wanted to escape the hood.

Johnny hopped out of the truck, walked

around to the passenger side, reeling a bit himself from the firewater he'd drunk earlier, and pulled Teddy's unconscious form from the vehicle. He slung Teddy over his shoulder and carried him into the house, dumping him on his old tattered couch, and then walked quickly back to the truck. Johnny wasn't done partying. He wanted to get back to the bridge and drink a little more.

Maybe that Jenny chick was drunk enough by now to suck him off in the woods. He was probably the only one on the basketball team who hadn't fucked her yet. He just wasn't good around girls, could never think of the right things to say. But rumor was that you could say just about anything and get into Jenny's panties once she had a few beers in her. Just thinking about it made Johnny swell in his shorts until they fit uncomfortably and he had to readjust himself. He started the truck and began driving back toward the bridge.

The moon was playing Hide 'n Seek tonight, ducking in and out of the clouds and taking all visibility with it whenever it disappeared, as Johnny chased visions of easy pussy up Winuba Lane. The darkness combined with the July heat felt oppressive, claustrophobic, as if he were driving through some damp underground cave and the night was solid walls closing in on all sides. Johnny was having a hard time keeping the truck on the road. In addition to the lack of streetlights, a dense fog had settled, further obscuring the road but thankfully cooling the air. Johnny rolled down the windows to let in the breeze. He leaned his head out of the car as the cool, damp air blew over his face and through his long shoulder-length hair. He could only see a yard or two ahead of his truck and was driving mostly from memory.

Johnny kept thinking about the pack of skinwalkers Teddy'd said he'd seen following them. He'd never known Teddy to be superstitious. He'd never heard him speak about any of the old myths before. Teddy didn't do sweat lodges or visit the Shaman. As far as Johnny knew, Teddy didn't even go to church. Neither did Johnny. But the anxiety in Teddy's voice had been real. He had really believed he'd seen something following them. Maybe he had seen something. Probably just a hallucination created by the mushrooms. Still, Johnny was getting spooked.

He felt foolish but kept checking the road for signs of wolves and shapeshifters. When he saw Howard climbing onto the bridge dripping wet, he didn't think much of it. It was just good ole Howie partying on the bridge. He'd probably fallen into the stream. He never could hold his alcohol. But then Johnny remembered that Howard had fallen into the water last night, not the stream but the river, and he hadn't crawled back out. Johnny was planning to attend his funeral tomorrow. He slowed down to get a closer look as he watched his dead friend climb over the railing and drop down onto the road. He had moss or weeds in his hair, and water puddled at his feet as it cascaded from his clothes.

Howard's skin was a pale greenish pallor mottled with blue veins and splotches of ruptured capillaries. His eyes were yellow and rheumy and looked as if they had deflated and sunken back into his skull. His tongue had turned black and hung from his mouth. A scream clawed its way up Johnny's throat as he finally realized what he was seeing. An owl flew past his windshield, and he jerked the steering wheel. Before he could correct his course, he swerved into the guardrail, smashing through it and hurtling down into the stream.

His face shattered the windshield, knocking three of his front teeth down his throat, crushing his nose, and splitting open his forehead as the front of his truck impacted with the rocks below. His body continued through the windshield, sliding across the hood of the truck and slamming face first into the water. Blood ran down his face and into his eyes. His vision began to fade but not before he saw the children swimming toward him. Their tiny hands reached out of the water, groping for him, pulling him under.

Johnny never struggled, even when he tried to inhale and his mouth and nostrils filled with water, breathing it into his lungs. He closed his eyes, slowly losing consciousness, drowning in a mere six inches of water.

CHAPTER 6

His face was pressed into the couch cushions when Teddy awoke, and his mouth and chin were wet with his own saliva. He had no idea how he'd gotten home but assumed one of his friends had driven him. Probably Johnny. Johnny always had his back, even when Teddy was making an ass of himself.

A little drummer boy was doing a solo in his head, and it felt like he had decided to experiment with speed metal. Johnny could feel it pounding from his temples to his molars. A fast, steady rhythmic pulse that Teddy knew, even as intoxicated as he was, had something to do with his heart. Something that was obviously not good. His pulse was way too fast, way too hard. He felt like he was minutes away from a heart attack.

Teddy had read about people having heart attacks on coke, especially athletes. A guy from their high school who'd gone to LA to play college ball had collapsed and died on the court after smoking crack in the locker room just last year. But Teddy had always assumed that type of thing only happened if you freebased. He'd always thought snorting it was safe. But now it felt like both his brain and his heart were seconds away from bursting.

Teddy didn't know why he'd snorted it in the first place. He rarely touched the stuff. The only time Teddy ever used coke was when Jenny was around. She was the only one he knew who could afford it. Crack was cheap enough, but that shit scared him. So did meth. Usually he stuck to beer and weed or painkillers, the occasional hit of acid on a Friday night after a game just for fun. But he'd been feeling reckless tonight, maybe even suicidal. He'd done every drug he could get his hands on.

The way his heart was hammering in his chest, it felt like he was about to join his friend. He needed something to calm his heart down, some downers or something. He still couldn't believe

Howard was dead. Then Teddy remembered what he'd seen under the bridge. Howard had been down there, alive. He was probably playing some kind of joke on all of them. Howard had always had a fucked-up sense of humor. He'd once put a rattlesnake in Johnny's bed and didn't understand why Johnny had gotten so mad. The idea that the thing might have killed him had never occurred to Howard. But maybe Howard wasn't just fucking with them. Maybe he was in some kind of trouble. Maybe he needed their help.

Teddy pulled himself up from the couch onto legs that felt like pillars of cement. His feet were numb and tingly. He wondered if that was another symptom of an impending cardiac arrest or if he had just cut off his circulation somehow when he'd passed out face down, ass up on the old sofa. He stumbled into the coffee table and spilled over it, hitting the vinyl floor forehead first and almost knocking himself unconscious. His teeth clashed together, biting into his tongue. Teddy's eyes moistened with tears, and he rolled over onto his back, reeling in pain, blood filling his mouth. He spit a wad of bloody phlegm onto the floor as he struggled back to his feet, holding his mouth.

"Fuck! That hurt."

He climbed off the floor and snatched up his dad's car keys, then stumbled out into the garage and collapsed behind the wheel of his dad's Dodge Charger. He turned the key in the ignition and listened to the sound of the motor purr. It was like a lullaby, like listening to his mother's heartbeat. He turned on the radio and waited for a moment, trying to sober up before driving back to the bridge. They were doing some kind of Michael Jackson tribute on the radio, and Teddy closed his eyes and listened to a young Mickey J sing about a girl who was now out of his life. As much as he hated to admit it, that freakish sonofabitch sure could sing. The slow, soft voice soon put him to sleep.

In his dreams, he was driving down Winuba Lane back to the bridge. When he got there, Johnny and Howard were waiting for him. They were skinny-dipping in the shallow stream, and little, pale, black-eyed babies floated in the water around them. They were all smiling, waving for Teddy to come join them. Teddy stripped off his clothes and jumped in.

CHAPTER 7

Her skin undulated, rippling with activity. It felt like legions of parasites were seething within her, worming their way through her flesh. Mika scratched at her forearms, trying to claw them out. She pulled her nightshirt over her head and scratched at her chest and stomach, leaving welts. "What the fuck? Oh my God!"

Something long and thin wriggled in a fast serpentine motion up her arm and across her chest, writhing its way down her torso to her belly. Mika clawed at her navel, trying to pull it out of her gut. She scratched violently at her arms and legs. Her skin felt like it was going to crawl right off. Mika could feel thousands of tiny … things … writhing and slithering, squirming up her legs, over her stomach, chest, arms, face. She dug her nails into her skin, gouging long rivulets in her flesh that quickly welled with blood. She tore off her bra and panties and raked her nails across her breasts, clawing at her nipples. She looked down and saw hundreds of pale, squiggling larvae boiling out of her vagina.

"Oh fuck! Maggots! They're inside me! They're inside of me!" Mika tried to scoop them out handful after handful. The feel of their slimy little bodies swarming between her thighs, up inside her, between her fingers as she thrust her hand deep into her sex, trying desperately to excavate the fly larva from her womanhood made her stomach threaten to revolt. She felt lightheaded. The room spun and darkened. Mika collapsed onto her pillow and allowed the darkness to suck her under.

The smell of sweat and beer, blood and semen, roared in Mika's nostrils. She felt rough whiskers brush her cheeks, and then a smothering weight crushed her into the mattress. Her eyes flew open. Uncle Jeff's battle-scarred face loomed above her, inches from her own, leaking blood and snot from his nose, drooling pink saliva onto her neck and breasts.

"Hello, little muffin. Did you miss your Uncle Jeff?"

She screamed long and loud as she struggled to free herself from beneath the disgusting pedophile. She punched and scratched at his face, wanting to tear him apart, to kill him the way her dad should have done a year ago.

Her mother burst into the room. Mika was writhing on the bed, still screaming, punching, and kicking. "Mika! Mika!"

"What the hell are you screaming about?" her dad yelled. "You're waking the whole damn house up! Will you be quiet! Shut the hell up, girl! I've got to go to work in the morning. Will you shut that girl up, woman?"

The sound of her father's voice cut through her terror. Mika opened her eyes again and saw her mother kneeling over the bed. Her uncle was gone. Mika looked around the room in a panic.

Her father stood in the doorway, glaring angrily at her. "What the hell was all that noise for?"

"I-I had a bad dream."

"A bad dream? You woke the whole house up because of a damn nightmare?" Her father's angry, unsympathetic words pummeled her like fists.

"I thought it was … It felt so real."

Her mom put a hand to her forehead to check for a fever. "Have you been taking your medication?"

Mika rolled over and turned her back to her mother without responding.

"Answer your mother! Did you hear her ask you a question?"

Mika knew that if she didn't answer, her father would get the belt and beat her. She didn't care. She had no more fear left for him. There were too many other things to be afraid of. Worse things than her father's drunken temper. She curled up into a ball as the first lash of the belt cracked across her bare back.

CHAPTER 8

The smell of bacon filled the house. Beneath it was a sweet buttery smell Mika associated immediately with her mother's homemade biscuits. She pulled herself from the bed, wincing as the scabs and scratches on her legs, arms, stomach, chest, neck, and face sang out in agony. Blood dotted her sheets from where her nails had punctured her skin.

Mika remembered the maggots she'd seen seething in her sex and quickly checked herself. There was nothing there but more scratches and welts. It had been another hallucination. Pain lanced across her back where her father's belt had scored her flesh.

The bright morning light speared through the

sheet that hung over her window in place of a curtain, penetrating her eyes and stabbing into her skull. Her head felt as if it was splitting in two. She closed her eyes and covered them with her hand to block the harsh sunlight. She stumbled toward her dresser and snatched a pair of shorts and a tank top from her drawer, wriggling into them, eager to get to the kitchen for breakfast.

Mika staggered out of her room and down the hall. The smell of bacon intensified, and her salivary glands went into overdrive. She could hear the sound of plates tinkling. It sounded like she had arrived just in time. They must have been setting the table. Mika stumbled into the kitchen, still shielding her eyes from the morning sun, squinting and yawning.

"What's for breakfast?"

"You missed it. We tried to wake you up, but you wouldn't even open your eyes."

Mika blinked against the glare of sunlight through the kitchen window and stared around the room in astonishment. Her brother was just getting up from the table, carrying an empty plate. Her father had already left for work, and her mother was standing at the sink washing the dishes.

"You didn't save me a plate?"

"Cliff wanted seconds, and since you were asleep, I wasn't going to let him go hungry."

Her brother smiled wide and winked at her. "Ay, you snooze, you lose," he said.

"You bastard."

"Watch your mouth, young lady! You should have woken up with the rest of us."

Mika rolled her eyes. "It's the summer, Mom. Nobody outside of this house gets up earlier than ten."

"They do if they want pancakes," her brother teased.

"There were pancakes? Mom! I should kick your ass, Cliff."

"You can try."

"Both of you stop it! You can scramble yourself an egg if you're hungry."

"Gee, thanks!" Mika replied as she plopped down into one of the metal-framed, vinyl-covered kitchen chairs. The legs were slightly bent, and the chair wobbled, almost pitching her over, which brought a volley of laughter from her little brother.

"I swear, Cliff. You had better watch yourself, boy."

"Just because you can't sit in a chair, don't take it out on me."

"This chair is fucked up."

"It's always been fucked up, but you're the only one who almost kills herself in it every morning." He laughed again, and Mika hissed.

"Just leave me alone, boy. I had a rough night."

"She had a bad dream last night," her mother offered.

"What was it about?"

"You don't want to know. What did you do last night?"

"I went to a party."

"A party? How does he get to go to parties? I couldn't go to parties when I was his age."

"Your father said it was okay. Besides, it's different now than when you were his age."

"What's changed in two years?"

"It's not that things have changed …"

"It's just that he's a boy and I'm a girl."

"Well, that does make a difference. Nobody is going to rape him or get him pregnant."

"That's not fair."

"Life isn't fair, dear. It just is what it is. Here, have some orange juice. I'll make you an egg. Next time, wake up so I don't have to dirty my pans all over again. You can wash them this time."

"Okay, Mom." She turned back to Cliff. "Whose

party was it?"

"Darrel Ray's little brother, Tommy. He just turned fourteen."

"Darrel Ray? The drug dealer?"

"He's not a drug dealer."

"He cooks up meth in his bathtub. There are dope fiends all over the place. It's like a damn crack house over there."

"You ought to know," Cliff whispered.

Mika glared murderously at him and mouthed the words "Fuck you."

Cliff smiled at her and chuckled.

Mika drank her orange juice in one gulp and jumped up from the table. "Never mind, Mom. I'm not hungry."

"Are you sure? What are you going to eat?"

"Nothing. I'll get lunch later."

Her mother looked concerned. "You should really eat something. You're getting too skinny as it is."

"I'm not hungry. Really. I'll get something later."

Mika scratched one of the welts on her arms, tearing off her scabs and causing her to bleed again. Her mother looked at the scratches all over her daughter and shook her head.

"You look terrible. What did you do to yourself?"

"I had a bad dream. That's all."

"What was it about?"

Mika remembered her Uncle Jeff drooling on her and trying to rape her in her bed. She thought about sparing her mother the details, but she wanted to shock her, maybe even hurt her a little. She knew her mother was still in denial over the rape, and she wanted to rub her face in it, force her mother to confront what her brother-in-law had done to her only daughter.

"I dreamt about Uncle Jeff."

It felt as if all the oxygen had left the room.

Her mother turned away and started scrubbing the dishes again. "Why did you dream about him?"

"It was a nightmare, Mom."

"Why would you be having nightmares about him?" Her mother had picked up a frying pan and was furiously scouring it with a plastic scrubber that was falling apart in her hand.

Her brother looked away as if embarrassed.

"Why the fuck do you think, Mom? Because he raped me."

Her mother scowled in disgust, and her shoulders tensed. "Oh, I don't think he raped you.

That's pretty harsh."

Mika couldn't believe what she was hearing. She picked a coffee cup up from the table and threw it hard against the floor, shattering it into a hundred jagged ceramic shards. Her mother jumped and let out a small squeal of surprise. She hurried over to the closet to retrieve a broom and dustpan, still avoiding her daughter's eyes as she began sweeping up the broken pieces. Mika stared at her mother, her mouth open, eyes wide and furious, filled with tears.

"He raped me!"

"Mika!"

"Look at me, Mom! Look at me!"

Her mother dropped the dustpan and leaned on the broom as she turned toward her daughter. Cliff was looking around the room as if searching desperately for a way out that would not take him past Mika.

"I know he touched you and fondled you, and that was wrong, but I don't think he raped you."

"He fucked me, Mom! He put his cock inside of me, and I bled. He came in my mouth. What the fuck do you call it if it wasn't rape?"

Her mother grimaced and placed the back of her hand to her lips, swallowing hard as if trying to stifle the urge to vomit, as if she, too, could taste Uncle Jeff's semen on her tongue, as if she, too, could feel him inside of her, tearing her hymen, grunting and sweating as she struggled beneath him. Cliff looked as if he was near panic. He ran out of the room with a stricken look on his face. Mika sneered at her mother and shook her head in disgust. She held up her hand, palm out, dismissing her mother as she walked out of the room after her brother.

"Cliff! Wait!"

She caught up to him on the driveway. His back was turned, and he was breathing heavily, gasping for breath as if he had run a mile rather than a few yards. He was trembling when Mika put her hand on his shoulder.

"Cliff? What's wrong?"

His eyes were brimming with tears when he turned and hugged her, squeezing her tight. "I didn't know, Mika. I didn't know he was hurting you. I swear I didn't know."

Mika hugged him back, then cupped a hand under his chin and tilted his head up so she could see his face. With her other hand she wiped away his tears. "It's okay, Cliff. It wasn't your fault. There wasn't anything you could do."

Cliff turned his head away. "I saw him."

"You saw him? When?"

Cliff nodded. "Last night when I was walking home from the party. I saw him down by the creek in back of Darrel and Tommy's house. He was standing there naked. He kept asking me to come swimming with him, but I got freaked out and just left. But I saw him before too." He hugged Mika tighter and buried his face in her shoulder.

She cupped his head in her hands and raised his head again until their eyes met. "What do you mean you saw him before?"

"I-I saw you … I saw him on top of you. I didn't know. I thought it was okay. I thought you were both just playing, having fun. I-I …"

"What?"

"I watched you."

"You what?"

"I watched you."

Mika let Cliff go and pushed him away from her. She walked down the driveway to the street, staggering as if she were sleepwalking.

"I'm sorry. I didn't know. I didn't know he was hurting you. I thought you liked it."

Mika didn't respond. She kept walking. She didn't know where she was going. She just knew she had to get away from Cliff … before she killed him.

She had walked less than a block when she ran into Jenny heading toward her. Her long blonde hair wasn't in cornrows anymore and looked like it had been professionally styled, shampooed, and blown dry. It looked gorgeous, like a movie star's hair. Long, golden locks flowed across her shoulders and down her back. But even as beautiful as her hair was, Jenny still looked like hell. She was crying, and mascara ran down her face like black tears. A cigarette dangled from her lip, looking like it was about to tumble out of her mouth. In one hand, she held a Red Bull energy drink, sipping between drags.

The feeling of dread that washed over Mika was overwhelming. She didn't want to hear what Jenny had to say. She didn't know if she could stand any more bad news.

Jenny swallowed the last of her Red Bull, then crushed the can and tossed it aside. She took a long drag from her cigarette before she spoke. "Teddy's dead. He fell asleep in his garage, in his car. The engine was running. He-he suffocated. Carbon monoxide poisoning or some shit."

Mika was stunned.

"What the fuck is going on?"

"Johnny's dead too. He ran his truck off the road, into the river. He drowned. It must have happened last night after he drove Teddy home."

"He drowned in that little-ass stream?"

Jenny shrugged. "He got knocked unconscious when he was thrown through the windshield, I guess. He must have landed face first in the water and just never woke up."

Mika felt the world start to spin again. She felt dizzy and reached out for Jenny to steady herself.

"Wait a minute. If John drove Teddy home, then what was Teddy doing sitting in his car?"

Jenny shrugged again and wiped the tears from her eyes, leaving ebon streaks and smears on her cheeks. "I don't know. Maybe he was going to go out to buy some more beer or score some more drugs. The funeral is tomorrow for both of them."

"And Howard's funeral is today. Three funerals in two days. Something ain't right. Something is seriously not right."

Jenny just shook her head and wiped more black tears from her eyes. "People die all the time around here. Car accidents, drug overdoses, domestic violence, hunting accidents. It's fucked up, but shit happens."

Mika shook her head. "No. This is different. Something ain't right. Something is just wrong about all of this."

Mika looked at the ground as if trying to find something she'd lost. She scratched her scalp and then her arms. She imagined she could feel Jenny's eyes crawling over her like insects. She began to scratch harder. She looked at her arms and saw things wriggling and slithering around beneath her skin just like last night. The maggots were back inside her again. She could feel them moving through her arm like large tadpoles swimming through her bloodstream. She looked at the welts that had now scabbed over where she had clawed at her skin. The welts began to separate, to split open. The scabs ripped and bled again as the wounds reopened and stretched wide like mouths with bleeding pink gums.

Within the gaping wounds, Mika could see things moving around. She dug her fingers into the widening gashes and pulled out two round white orbs. She rolled them around in her hand until the two tiny eyeballs were staring right at her. She screamed and dropped them to the ground, backing away quickly. She looked back at her arm, and it was bursting with eyeballs, bubbling up out of the lacerations in her forearms. She screamed again and began tearing into her arm with her nails, trying to dig out the eyes.

Jenny tackled her and seized Mika's wrists with both hands.

"Stop! Stop it! You're hallucinating again!"

Mika pulled her arms free of Jenny's grasp and raised them up so she could see them. The welts on her arms were bleeding again, but they hadn't torn open and they weren't full of eyeballs. She covered her face with both hands and dropped her head.

"Fuck. I think this shit is getting worse."

"Wow. I thought you were going to open a vein."

Mika dropped her hands from her face, which was now stained with blood. She sat on the ground with her arms bleeding into the dirt. She stared at Jenny as if she didn't recognize her.

"We need to get cleaned up. The funeral is in an hour."

Mika turned her head, no longer looking at Jenny when she spoke. She stared at her arm, picking the dirt and grass out of her wounds. "I'm not going. I'm going to see my father."

"Isn't he at work? What do you want to see him for?"

"No, not that prick. I'm talking about my real dad."

"Joshua?"

"Yeah. He's supposed to be some kind of medicine man, right? Maybe he knows something about all this shit."

"I didn't know he was a medicine man. I mean, I don't know shit about him except that he's on the tribal council. Neither do you, really."

"Well, I heard somewhere that he was a shaman or something. Maybe I imagined it. Even if he's not, he's on the tribal council and he's Indian. It's an Indian legend. He's got to know something about it."

"Isn't Indian politically incorrect? Don't they call themselves Native Americans now?"

"Not around here they don't."

"True. Well, let's go then."

"You're coming with me? You're not going to the funeral?"

"Nah, I was just coming here to see if you wanted to get high. Hearing about Teddy kind of fucked me up. I scored some meth. You want to do it with me before we go?"

Mika's eyes lit up at the mention of her favorite street pharmaceutical. "I'm broke, though. I can't even afford the pink shit, and I'm fiending like fuck. I was hoping I could jack off one of the boys on the reservation for a hit."

Jenny shook her head. "You're crazy. Besides, they'd want more than a handjob these days. You'd fuck around and get gang raped. They'd at least want a blowjob. You know I wouldn't charge you. Not today, anyway. You look like you could use a hit. You can hook me up some other time, or you can jack me off if it'll make you feel better. It would certainly make *me* feel better. I haven't gotten laid in days."

In truth, Jenny had never charged her for drugs, though Mika had paid her anyway when she could afford to. She never wanted it to seem like she was taking advantage of her wealthy friend the way everybody else did.

"Thanks. You really think I would have gotten raped?"

"You never know."

"You know, I heard Gina got gang raped by the gazebo last month."

Jenny shook her head and laughed. "Is that what she said happened? I hope she ain't going to the cops or nothing. 'Cause that's bullshit. I was there. She was all fucked up on 'shrooms and X and she just started sucking off Nate and his brothers. She just started grabbing all their cocks, and then she drops to her knees and pulls Nate's cock out and starts sucking it. You know, big redneck Nate?" Jenny said.

"Nate Michealson with the hair and acne all down his back who always smells like BO?"

"The one with the long armpit hair. Yeah, it was him, his brother Frank, his oldest brother, Sam with all the tattoos. Jake was there too. You know Jake who plays guitar at the saloon? The one who dropped out of school last year?"

"She fucked them all? That's rugged!"

"Yup. I was there, and Trina Lassiter was there, and they wanted us to join in."

"Did you?"

"Fuck no! I wouldn't let none of them nasty fucks touch me. I don't think Nate and his brothers even bathe. Besides, I like Indian boys."

"I can't really say I've ever known you to discriminate. You just like Indian boys because your dad is prejudice against them and you like pissing him off."

"Yeah, and they've got big dicks." Jenny winked at Mika with a mischievous grin on her face. She licked her lips suggestively.

"Some do, but some definitely don't. Just like anybody else."

"You've just been fucking the wrong ones. You need to get around more," Jenny replied, flicking her hair back out of her face with one hand.

"I'm not really trying to put numbers on the board. It ain't like it's a damn contest," Mika said with obvious distaste. "But anyway, back to Gina. So, what did y'all do? Just stand there and watch?"

"What else could we do?"

"I don't know. You could have left or took her with you. I mean, if you knew she was fucked up. You should have stopped her."

"I didn't want to leave her alone, but she was a big girl and she knew what she was doing. They did fuck the shit out of her, though. They didn't use condoms or nothing. They were taking turns. One would cum in her, and then the next would stick his dick right in there after him like it wasn't nothing. It was nasty."

Mika felt herself getting aroused and was surprised by it. A moist warmth spread between her thighs, making her feel uncomfortable and embarrassed. Her cheeks turned red. She wanted to hear more, even as disgusting as it was, but didn't want Jenny to know it was turning her on. Frank and Sam might have been butt ugly, but Nate and Jake didn't look bad. Plus, the idea of being fucked by more than one guy had always turned her on, though she was in no hurry to try it. Some things, Mika thought, ought to remain fantasies.

"Jake came all over her face," Jenny said with obvious relish.

"Okay, that's enough. Ewww. I didn't need to hear that." Mika grimaced.

"I kind of like it when guys cum on my face. It makes me feel all nasty, like a porno star."

"Jenny! I really don't want to hear this. I don't want to think of you with some guy's jizz dripping off your forehead. You are rugged, girl. That shit is gross! I can't even look at you now. Let's just go somewhere and get high before we go. You sure you okay goin' to the rez with me? I mean, two white girls walking through there by ourselves might look weird."

"We'll be fine. Good thing you're half Indian. Even if your dad is too stupid to figure it out, everyone else knows it."

"Really? You think everyone knows?"

Jenny laughed. "Oh yeah. Trust me. Eeeeeeveryone knows. It's obvious when you look at you. You don't even look like your dad. You look Indian."

"You mean Native American."

Jenny smirked. "Yeah, that too."

The girls headed down the street. After they'd gone a few blocks, Jenny walked them across an overgrown field with grass and weeds that were nearly waist high. Mika followed, excited, knowing she was about to get high and happy she wouldn't have to risk getting raped to do it. Mika felt the smile spread slowly across her face as she watched Jenny lean against a tree and take out a small ball of aluminum foil. She opened it, revealing the gritty white substance within. When Mika looked up from the drugs, she saw that Jenny was smiling too.

"This is the good stuff. That pink shit is weak."

She held a lighter beneath the foil and inhaled.

"You ever smoke it before? It gets you high quicker than snorting it."

"I did once at a party. It reminded me too much of smoking crack."

Jenny closed her eyes, enjoying the rush, still holding the lighter and the foil. "You ever smoked crack before?"

Mika shook her head.

"You should try that sometime too. Just because

spics and Blacks do it doesn't mean it's bad. It's the most powerful high I've ever had."

"Really?" Mika asked, curious but still unconvinced. She'd seen crackheads and crackwhores when she'd gone to LA with her family. That was not a lifestyle she was eager to emulate.

"Oh yeah. I wanted to fuck like crazy, though, and there was nobody around. I was alone in my room. So I went into my mom's room and found her vibrator. I must have made myself cum about twenty times. My pussy was sore as hell the next day."

"You were smoking crack in your own house and using your mom's vibrator?"

"My mom don't care. She's always so high, I doubt she even remembers she has a daughter, and Dad is always too busy with his horses. The only way I could get his attention would be to slap a saddle on and run around the stable. He has bigger life insurance policies on his stallions than he does on me."

"That sucks. Your parents are old as fuck, though. They probably just don't have the energy for kids anymore."

"I ain't askin' them to push me on a swing or

play fuckin' catch with me. They don't even talk to me! I don't fucking exist to them! I get in trouble, and they just pay the bills, give me some weak-ass punishment that they never enforce, and go back to ignoring me."

"At least they don't beat the shit out of you like my dad does."

"I'd prefer getting my ass kicked to being ignored. At least you know he-he c-cares." Jenny's eyes welled with tears. Her face was a mask of pain. Her voice cracked with emotion when she spoke.

Mika felt her own eyes begin to tear up, not for Jenny but for the feelings Jenny's sorrows were stirring up within her. Mika's own parents weren't exactly loving and attentive. They hadn't wanted her any more than Jenny's parents had.

"I don't know if it means he cares. I think beating the shit out of things is the only way he knows how to handle problems. He slapped my mom once right in front of me."

"My mom and dad don't even talk to each other. They don't fuck anymore. Mom has a boyfriend that comes to our house and fucks the shit out of her while my dad is home, and he doesn't even care. Dad is fucking half the widows and bored housewives in town. He'll stick his dick in anything. I don't know how anyone can fuck that wrinkled old bastard. Can you imagine sucking a wrinkled dick?"

"Eww! Hell no!" Mika said. Her eyes were glued to the off-white substance in the aluminum foil that Jenny was still holding in her hand. It looked like a small lump of raw sugar. She wanted to end this conversation so she could get high. She just didn't know what Jenny wanted her to say. Jenny knew how fucked up her parents were. What was the point in dwelling on it? That's what drugs were for. Tune in. Turn on and burn out and all that shit.

"My mom knows I steal her drugs. She doesn't care. The guy she's fucking, he's her damn doctor. He fucks her and writes her prescriptions for whatever she wants. And she just sits in her room watching soap operas, talk shows, and reality shows until he comes back to fuck her fat ass again or until her girlfriends pick her up to go shopping. That's all she does is shop, eat, fuck, sleep, and get high. I walk right in there and take the drugs out of her medicine cabinet, take money out of her purse, and she just smiles at me and waves me away like I'm annoying her."

"Well, your mom is a little ..."

"Old, obese, and overly medicated? That's her own damn fault. If she gave a fuck about me, she'd get off the Vicodin and get on an exercise program."

"Didn't she break her back or something?"

"She's got a ruptured disk and arthritis in her vertebrae. The doctors gave her Vicodin for the pain, and she fell in love with the shit. She eats those pills like fucking candy. She's like a fucking zombie. That shit numbed her mind right along with her pain."

"I'm sure they still love you, though. They're just a little selfish. They had you after all their other kids were grown. They were ready to enjoy life without kids, and you popped up and ruined their party. They probably didn't know what to do with you."

Jenny's eyebrows furrowed, and her mouth twisted into a snarl. It was a rare moment of emotion for Jenny, whose emotions generally ran from listlessness to arousal to euphoria and back. Seeing her sad or angry was rare indeed.

"What the fuck? Are you on their side? You make it sound like it was my fault for being born!"

Mika smiled lopsidedly and patted Jenny on the shoulder to calm her. "I'm just keepin' it real.

You were a mistake just like I was. My dad wanted a boy. Your dad wanted a pony."

Mika held the lighter under the foil until the methamphetamine inside began to burn. She inhaled deeply, and soon, the rush hit her, adrenaline and endorphins rushing through her veins like a burst of rocket fuel. Her eyes sparkled with energy. Her pupils dilated until very little of the irises were visible. They looked like two bullet holes in her skull. She bounced from one foot to the other. Her jaw twitched and her hands clenched and unclenched. She rolled her head in a circle to loosen the tendons in her neck like a prize fighter waiting for the bell to sound to begin the first round. She felt invincible, ready to take on the world.

"Yeah, well, fuck 'em both," Jenny replied. "As long as they keep giving me money, who needs love?"

"Was that a question or a statement? 'Cause I think you already know the answer."

Mika handed the foil and lighter to Jenny, who added another rock of meth and heated it with the lighter, inhaling the last of the crystal. They both stood under the tree breathing hard and grinning stupidly. Jenny reached out almost absentmindedly and ran her hand slowly over Mika's small pear-shaped breasts.

Mika's nipples hardened, and she felt small jolts of sensation prickling at the root of her. She let out a sigh that seemed to come from somewhere deep in her soul. She reached out and cupped Jenny's voluptuous breasts in her hands, rubbing her thumbs across the bullet-sized nipples poking through her T-shirt. She smiled at Jenny nervously, and Jenny reached out and cupped the back of Mika's head in her hand, drawing her closer until their lips met. This time, there was no hesitation, no apprehension. They kissed deeply, tongues dueling and dancing. Mika sucked Jenny's tongue, twirling her tongue around it, and then sucked her bottom lip before slipping her own tongue into Jenny's mouth, where Jenny eagerly returned the favor.

Mika felt Jenny's cool palms sliding slowly beneath her shirt, over her stomach, and up to her breasts. Jenny's hands were all over her, rubbing lightly over her breasts, softly pinching her nipples, sliding around and up her back and down to her ass, cupping Mika's small buttocks and squeezing them firmly.

The few awkward boys Mika had experimented

with in the past year had never made her feel this way. They had never touched her the way Jenny was touching her. Softly, tenderly, caressing rather than groping. Their hands had been rough, fumbling, artless. Jenny's hands were slow and patient; each touch began to gradually build Mika to the type of climax she'd only experienced at her own hand. Mika wondered if maybe she was enjoying this too much. She didn't want to be a lesbian. She liked boys. But she didn't want Jenny to stop.

Jenny's heavy, humid breath against Mika's neck was driving her crazy. Jenny's fingertips were tickling their way down Mika's stomach to her hips and then to the top of her jeans. Jenny undid the first button. Then Mika quickly unzipped her pants and shoved Jenny's hands down into her panties, into the moist warmth between her thighs.

"Oh, fuck that feels good," Mika whispered between moans.

Mika pulled Jenny's shirt up to reveal her friend's huge breasts, which were easily a D-cup or larger. She scooped Jenny's breasts out of her bra, squeezed them firmly, then bent down and sucked one of the girl's nipples into her mouth. She licked and sucked from one nipple to the other, buried her face between Jenny's breasts, and inhaled the girl's fresh baby powder scent as Jenny's fingers worked magic between Mika's thighs. Mika could hear Jenny moaning as she flicked her tongue quickly over the girl's swollen nipples. As Jenny's fingers worked expertly between Mika's thighs, bringing her closer and closer to orgasm, she had to resist the urge to bite down on the girl's nipple.

"Oh fuck. Oh shit. Don't stop. Oh fuck!" Mika felt like she was about to rattle apart. Her thighs shook. Her stomach quivered. Her nerve endings felt like they had been plugged into a wall socket.

Jenny lifted Mika's head from her breasts and kissed her forehead, then her nose, her cheeks, her eyelids, and finally her lips, another long, soul deep kiss that neither of them wanted to break. Mika unzipped Jenny's shorts and slid her hand down into the girl's soaking wet panties.

They stood there, leaning against a tree in the middle of an empty field. A cool breeze ruffling the verdant grass. Storm clouds roiling above their heads, the Sierra Nevada looming majestically in the background. Kissing passionately. Feverishly masturbating one another to orgasm. Mika came first. Her body began to lose all control, jerking and hitching. Tears ran down Mika's face, and she let out a low animalistic moan that was part ecstasy, part anguish. Jenny came next. She kissed Mika all over her face as she held the girl's hand tight to her sex with both hands.

Jenny withdrew her hand from Mika's shorts. Her fingers glistened, wet with vaginal fluid. Mika watched transfixed as Jenny brought her fingers to her lips and licked each one.

"I've been wanting to know what you taste like all week. Mmmmm. Now I know."

Mika grabbed the girl and kissed her, tasting her own juices on her friend's tongue. Then she pulled her hand from Jenny's shorts and sucked them, feeling that pleasant tingling between her thighs again. She kissed Jenny once more.

"I want to taste you for real," Jenny said, staring deep into Mika's eyes while running her hands down the front of her pants.

"I love you," Mika replied, meaning it more than she had ever realized. She hugged Jenny close and sobbed with her head on the girl's ample bosom. Mika felt her friend's fingers comb through her short, inch long hair, then felt the girl's lips as Jenny kissed the top of her head.

"I love you too, Mika."

Mika shrugged out of her shorts and pulled her

shirt off over her head, then lay down in the tall grass. Jenny did the same, her large breasts flopping out of her bra as she unhooked it and pulled off her T-shirt. Mika held out her arms for her, and Jenny laid down on top of her, kissing Mika's lips and then her neck, her small tits, pausing to suck each nipple. Mika moaned with anticipation as Jenny kissed her way down her stomach to the light trail of hair that led to her sex. Mika's back arched and she bit her lower lip as Jenny sucked her clitoris, swirling her tongue around it until it swelled and pulsated, flicking her tongue across it until Mika cried out. Mika's body tensed and began to convulse as another orgasm, the most powerful one she'd ever experienced, shook her like a kite in a storm. She felt Jenny's tongue wriggle its way inside her as Mika rode the wave of orgasms through its cataclysmic aftershocks. Mika looked up at the sky and watched the dark clouds above morph into familiar faces.

She saw Howard's face smiling down at her. She saw Teddy and Johnny and then Uncle Jeff, dark and threatening. He was smiling too, but it looked more like a snarl. Then his face contorted into a mask of hate. Teddy and Johnny stopped smiling. So did Howard. The expressions on their faces twisted into grimaces of pain and terror. All at once, they began to scream. The sound was deafening. Mika covered her ears and screamed too. Jenny's tongue was still lapping greedily at Mika's clit, and another orgasm tore through her, sending her body into a seizure as waves of pure pleasure wracked her body. The faces in the clouds dissipated. The echo of their screams faded into the distance. Mika swallowed hard and let out a long, slow breath.

Jenny's lips were drenched in Mika's juices when she rose from between her thighs. Mika sat up and kissed her friend, once again tasting her own juices on the girl's lips.

"Did you like that?" Jenny asked. She was smiling, excited, but she also looked worried, afraid that she hadn't done it right, eager for Mika's approval.

"Oh my God. That was fucking incredible!"

"Do you want me to do it again?"

"Later. First, I want to do you."

Still panting and out of breath, Mika rolled Jenny over and dropped down between her thick thighs. She licked and sucked Jenny's clit, fluttering her tongue over the clit the way Jenny had done to her. She slid a finger up inside of her, then two, then three, and began fucking the girl with her hand as she continued to lick and suck her clit. A light drizzle of rain fell, momentarily cooling them both off and raising goosebumps on their skin. Jenny was moaning and crying out. A flood of juices, thick like nectar, poured from Jenny's sex across Mika's tongue as her body began to buck and thrash. Mika didn't stop. She held Jenny down, wrapping her arms around the big girl's thighs and burying her face in her sex, making circles with her tongue, swirling it around her clit like she was licking a lollipop as Jenny came again and again and again.

The rain stopped, and a few rays of sunlight peeked out from between the black clouds. Mika rolled off Jenny and onto her back. She watched angels, ghosts, and snarling demons chase each other through the heavens, unmoved by their antics. The demons all looked like her uncle, and they all had huge erections. The angels looked like Mika. Mika had to restrain herself from yelling at them to run faster. This was one of those rare visions that Mika knew was obviously in her head. More chimeras conjured by her diseased mind. When the little Jeff demons caught up to the angels, Mika turned away, not wanting to see their faces as they were raped and sodomized. The sounds were bad enough. She winced at the sound of flesh slapping against flesh and the grunts, groans, and anguished weeping that accompanied it.

Mika knew that the longer she went without taking her antipsychotic medication, the stronger the hallucinations would become. But she would rather see Uncle Jeff's face a hundred times a day than go back on those mind-numbing drugs. When she was on her medication, her mind felt like it was in slow motion, like her thoughts were weighted down, swimming through an ocean of mud like a dinosaur stuck in a tar pit. If her brother hadn't seen him too, it would have been easy to convince herself that she hadn't seen her uncle under the bridge either, that he had been just another hallucination. But Cliff had seen him too, right after Uncle Jeff had threatened to rape her brother in place of her.

Mika closed her eyes, shutting out the visions, and curled up next to her friend and lover. She rubbed Jenny's stomach, breasts, and neck softly as her body continued to quiver. They both lay in the grass, holding each other while the sweat and rain and their own sticky wet juices dried on their skin. They tried to calm their breathing and steady their galloping hearts. Mika ran her fingers through Jenny's hair and smiled at her.

"I'm in love with the town whore."

"I'm not the town whore. This is a town full of whores, and I ain't the worst of them by a long shot. And I love you too."

"So does this make us lesbians?"

"Probably. Is that such a bad thing?"

"I guess not. I mean, no guy ever made me feel like this, but then no one ever went down on me before."

"Really?"

"Nope. I was a virgin until a year ago. I went a little crazy after Uncle Jeff did what he did, and I slept with a few guys, but it was terrible. I was fucking Howard for a while until I threw up in his car after giving him head. Mike Reynolds fucked me in the back of his dad's pickup, and I almost scratched his face off when he tried to put it in my ass. It hurt like hell. Then there were a few drunken nights with Tony Vasquez and his cousin in the woods by the bridge."

"I know. I was there, remember? I was the one fucking his cousin most of the time while Tony was fucking you. We switched a few times, though. You know, I wanted to fuck you way back then. I always thought we'd wind up fucking while they both watched or joined in or something. I use to fantasize about it all the time."

"When did you stop?"

"After the other night by the bridge. Now I just fantasize about fucking you with no one else around. Sort of like we just did."

Mika blushed and turned away sheepishly.

"Was it … you know … as good as it was in your dreams?"

Jenny rolled on to her side and kissed Mika on the lips again. "It was better."

"Good."

"I can't believe that was the first time anyone ever went down on you. What a trip! And I can't believe those are the only guys you ever fucked. I mean, you certainly looked like you knew what you were doing when I used to watch you fuck Tony."

"That was it. Those are the only guys I ever fucked, and it was never like this. I never even came with any of them. I never felt like I was making love before."

"So what do we do now?" Jenny asked, then leaned over and kissed Mika on the nose. She ran the back of her hand over Mika's cheek as she stared into her eyes.

Mika sat up and groped for her clothes in the grass. She pulled her T-shirt back on and wriggled back into her panties.

"We go see my father."

Jenny stood up and began getting dressed also. "I mean, what do we do about us?"

"Nothing changes. We keep being friends. We keep hanging out together, getting high together …"

Mika could see the dejected look on Jenny's face. She ran her hand between Jenny's thighs, sliding a finger inside of her. Jenny gasped. A surprised smile burst onto her face.

"And we keep fucking."

Mika withdrew her finger and brought it to Jenny's lips. Jenny licked Mika's finger lovingly, savoring the taste of her own juices. She threw her head back and sighed. "I so want to fuck you again."

"I want you too, but we need to find out what's going on before more people start dying."

"Okay. Let's go see your dad then."

CHAPTER 9

Clifton Shaw had been spoiled by his father since the day he was born. He was his parents' first and only son. All of his dad's wasted dreams now rested on his shoulders. His father, Joe Shaw, had almost made it to the major leagues, and that "almost" haunted him to this day. When Clifton was born, his father had viewed it as his second chance at the big leagues. But as much as he didn't want to disappoint him, deep down, Cliff knew he would never be a major league baseball player. That was his father's dream, and though it would have been nice, Cliff knew that there were other kids more talented than him, even if his dad was too blind to see it. He thought no other kid on earth was better than his son. It was what dads were supposed to think about their children, but when it came to Cliff's sister Mika, it was the exact opposite. Mika had always gotten the short end of the stick when it came to their dad.

She got the beatings that Cliff should have gotten, and Cliff got the love, support, and attention denied his sister. Cliff had always felt guilty for it. And now he had failed his sister when she'd needed him the most. He had seen what Uncle Jeff had done to her, and he had done nothing. He had stood there watching while his sister was being raped. He had even gotten turned on. She hated him now. And he hated himself. He had to make it right somehow.

The sky was a dark gray that crackled with flashes of lightning as Cliff made his way back to the creek where he'd seen Uncle Jeff. He walked quickly, trying to get there before the rains began. He had his father's Browning A-bolt .22 rifle with a fully loaded magazine slung over his shoulder. When he saw his uncle again, he would do what his father should have done a year ago.

The sun broke through the clouds briefly, and Cliff sped up his pace, imagining pumping round after round into that pedophile's face. Then he would bury his uncle's body in the woods deep enough to conceal him, but not so deep that the coyotes and mountain lions couldn't get to him. By the time anyone found him, there would be almost nothing left. Cliff hated to think about destroying his daddy's rifle, but he knew he would have to. He'd seen enough cop shows on TV to know that if they managed to find his uncle's body and the Browning, a ballistics test would prove that the fatal bullet had come from his dad's weapon. But not if he ran a power drill down the barrel first. He had it all figured out. Now it was as simple as finding his uncle. He would take care of everything else from there. Uncle Jeff would never hurt anyone again.

Cliff reached Brockman Lane just as the rain began. This was where he'd seen his uncle standing naked in the creek. He pulled the Browning off his shoulder and checked the magazine, then jacked a round into the chamber.

"Uncle Jeff!" he called out as he walked down to the creek. He paused to listen for a reply but could hear nothing but the trickle of creek water and the pitter patter of bloated raindrops on the leaves overhead. He continued walking toward the creek.

Cliff soon found himself standing by the edge of the water. The rain was coming down harder, pounding the earth, leaving little divots in the muddy soil and drenching Cliff's clothing. He looked around, feeling foolish for thinking his uncle would still be down there skinny dipping in the creek a day later. He was about to turn around and head back to the road when he heard a high-pitched giggle. He whirled around quickly, thinking it had come from behind him. A white owl flew past him, startling him and almost causing him to lose his balance.

"Fuck! What the hell was that?"

He scanned the other side of the creek as rain bulleted down his forehead into his eyes. He could see nothing but more trees. Then he heard the unmistakable sound of children weeping. He wiped the rainwater from his eyes and squinted, trying to see through the downpour to spot whoever was down there crying, when he realized that the noise was coming from the creek, from the water itself. Cliff dropped the rifle onto a rock and waded out into the creek water, searching for the source of the sobs. He was waist deep in the creek when he saw the babies.

There was nearly a dozen of them bobbing along in the water. They all had black pupils that reminded Cliff of a barracuda that had swallowed his line once when he'd been fishing in Mexico with his dad. It had crawled up his line and almost bit him. It had those same flat, dead eyes, devoid of all warmth, that seemed to swallow the light and refuse to give it back. Their skin was fish belly white and wrinkled, as if it had never seen the sun, like something that had been underwater for years.

They stopped crying and began swimming toward him. They were smiling now, but their smiles held no more warmth than their cold, lifeless eyes. Something about those emotionless expressions made Cliff's blood freeze. Their mouths looked too big with too many teeth. There was something predatory about them, like a school of smiling piranha. And they were getting closer. He tried to run, slogging through the waist deep water, trying to get back onto land and away from the babies with the big teeth and black eyes.

The first bite was so much worse than he would have imagined. It bit clean through the muscle, down to the bone. Cliff cried out as the little baby began to thrash its body back and forth like a shark, shaking its head until it had torn out a large piece of his thigh. Blood filled the water, and that seemed to agitate the rest of them. They attacked en masse, and soon Cliff was engulfed by snarling, biting children.

"Owwww! Fuuuuck! Help! Heeeelp! Oh Fuck! Noooooo! Noooooooo!"

He punched at them and tried to pull them off as they tore piece after piece from his legs and torso. Blood poured from a dozen large, ragged avulsions the babies had torn in his flesh. He screamed again and again as his legs gave out and he splashed down into the water. The babies overwhelmed him, clawing at his face, biting into his throat, and digging their tiny hands into his eyes. Cliff thought he heard his uncle's voice just before he submerged beneath the rushing water, pulled down by the weight of the water babies, his flesh unmade by their savage little teeth. He felt his uncle's thin, wiry arm around his throat and smelled his rancid beer and tobacco breath.

"Your sister is next, Clifton. And it's all your fault. You should have saved her when you could."

Cliff tried to fight harder, to free himself so he could warn his sister, but the babies had eaten his muscles down to nothing and were already chewing into his organs. He could feel their hands and teeth worrying away at his insides, tearing him apart.

"I'm sorry," he whispered before his vocal chords were chewed out by tiny mouths, his lips torn from his face.

CHAPTER 10

The two girls walked quickly up Barlow Lane, holding hands and giggling, casting long love-struck glances at one another, truly happy for the first time in either of their lives. They both knew how dangerous it was for them to be on the reservation alone. Mika had never been to the reservation before unless she was accompanied by one of the Indian boys from her school, and even then, she'd get evil stares from the reservation girls who suspected her of trying to steal their men. The girls on the reservation hated Jenny even more because at seventeen, she already had a reputation for fucking any Indian boy she could get her hands on.

It had begun to rain again, only now, it was

coming down in sheets. Mika had to cover her eyes to peer through the deluge. The two girls skipped and splashed through the puddles, enjoying life as the rain washed over them and plastered their clothes to their skin. Mika was not wearing a bra, and her dark nipples stabbed through her shirt, which was now nearly transparent. Jenny's shirt was drenched as well, but she wore a bra beneath it, which afforded her some degree of modesty. Mika kept catching Jenny staring hungrily at her tits.

"Fuck, you look good."

Mika folded her arms across her chest and smiled. "I wish you weren't wearing a bra either. Then we'd be even."

Jenny reached beneath her shirt and unhooked her bra. She pulled it out through her shirt sleeve and tossed it into a puddle by the side of the road. Mika reached out and squeezed Jenny's nipples, which had hardened as well and were now as conspicuous as her own.

"I can't believe how much your tits turn me on," Jenny said. "I guess I really am a lesbian."

"Do you feel bad about us not going to Howard's funeral?"

The question stifled all the mirth between them.

The smile fell hard from Mika's face. She walked along staring at the ground for a while before she answered.

"I guess I should. I mean, I do a little."

"Do you think anyone will even remember them in a few years? I mean Howard, Teddy, and Johnny? Do you think we'll remember them when we're older?"

"They died young. That kind of thing sticks in people's minds. They're legends now, at least in this town, they are. We'll be telling our kids about them someday when we warn them about drinking and driving or using drugs. Just like the stories our parents told us about kids that died in the seventies and eighties. That's how it goes here. Everybody dies a legend in little shit towns like this. The more fucked up their deaths, the more they'll be remembered."

"What about us? Who's gonna remember us when we die?"

"I guess that depends on how we die."

A silence fell between them, heavy and funereal, like the closing of a casket or the slamming of a mausoleum door, as they both contemplated their own mortality. The sky darkened. Thunder rumbled overhead like the growl of some impossibly large beast. Blue-white flashes of electric fire fractured the heavens. Mika pulled Jenny closer.

"Can we make a stop real quick?" Jenny asked, pointing to a small house in the middle of an empty field. It was an old, brown, dilapidated single-story with weeds growing around it. The creek that wound through the reservation ran less than half a mile in back of it, and Mika could hear the tinkle of the water the closer they came to the building. Mika knew the house. It was Darrel and Tommy Ray's. A drug den. "I need to score some more meth. I don't really like the stuff all that much, but I know you do, and that shit sells like crazy around here."

Mika blushed. "You don't have to buy me any. I'm good."

"It's not just for you. I need to get some more to sell. Nobody can afford coke anymore, unless it's crack, but they are going nuts over this meth. I already sold all the stuff I bought yesterday. Come on. It'll be quick."

The two girls walked across the disheveled lawn as the rain continued to pour. Mud caked the bottom of their shoes as it sank into the earth. They swatted mosquitoes from their arms and faces and brushed aside weeds nearly as tall as them.

An old Buick sat rusting on cinderblocks halfway across the lawn, and a tire swing hung from a tree whose leaves were all brown despite the season. Broken toys littered the yard along with beer cans, empty bottles, and cigarette butts. They passed the occasional dirty diaper swarming with flies or pile of feces that looked more human than animal.

"This place is a real shithole," Mika said.

"Ever since Darrel's dad went to the penitentiary, this place has become like a crack house."

The rain had stopped by the time they reached Darrel's house. The front door hung open, dangling from a single hinge. The door jamb was completely busted out where the lock should have been. The door had been kicked in by cops and dope fiends so often they had just stopped replacing it. Mika and Jenny walked up the steps and into the house.

The floors were made of linoleum loaded with asbestos and covered in a layer of dust an inch thick. Rat and insect droppings were everywhere. There were a few tattered throw rugs tossed here and there. Beer cans were piled on the coffee tables and end tables along with empty pizza boxes and fast food wrappers. A mountain of clothes littered the floor. There were holes punched into the heavily graffitied walls. A cockroach struggled in a spider's web above the kitchen door. A baby no older than a year crawled out from behind the sofa, and Mika wrapped her arms around Jenny, squeezing her tight. She was about to scream when she realized that it was a real baby.

The baby looked too skinny, malnourished, and its diaper sagged, leaking piss and shit down the infant's leg as it crawled along the linoleum floor. Mika's stomach turned as she watched the baby sit down beside a candy wrapper that was crawling with roaches and begin picking the insects off one by one and shoving them into its mouth, chewing happily.

Mika slowly released her grip on Jenny's waist but kept hold of her hand as they walked around the cockroach-eating baby and made their way to the back bedroom.

Darrel Ray lounged on a mattress that sat on the floor with the two emaciated crack whores that helped make his product. A shotgun, a big revolver, and what looked like an Uzi submachine gun lay within easy reach by the filthy mattress. There was a chemistry set erected in the master bathtub. A dozen boxes of pseudoephedrine pills, a bottle of iodine, a bunch of old lithium batteries, a bottle of muriatic acid, a can of acetone, and methyl alcohol surrounded the tub. Everything a street pharmacist would need to cook meth.

"You still cooking that shit in your house? You gonna blow this place up one day," Jenny said.

Darrel's skin was pockmarked with bleeding sores that he'd been picking at for ages. Mika looked at her own arms where she'd scratched and picked at her skin and wondered how long before she looked as bad as Darrel Ray. He had the high cheekbones, dark tan complexion, and thick black hair of Paiutes but lacked his people's size, thanks to years of tweaking. When he smiled, his chapped lips pulled back, revealing a mouth nearly devoid of teeth. Most of them had long ago rotted away, leaving blackened holes in his gums. His arms and throat were mottled with at least three different pigments from where past chemical explosions had left severe burn scars.

"I don't even use that shit anymore. I use the shake and bake method now. I just put the cold pills and the rest of that shit in a milk jug, shake it for, like, twenty minutes, and cook that shit. It's easy as fuck. If you mutherfuckers weren't so chicken shit, you'd just make it yourself instead of bothering me for the shit. But as long as you're buyin', I'm sellin'."

"Keep it up and I just might go into business for myself."

Darrel snorted. "Bullshit. You don't got the heart. This shit could still explode on your ass if you shake it wrong and leave too much oxygen in there. You take the lid off too quickly. Anything can go wrong. Besides, this shit here is a big-time felony. Ten years minimum. I know you're not tryin' to do any time."

"How much you got?"

"How much you need?"

"I got, like, five hundred bucks."

"That'll buy you four and a half grams."

"That's it? It was thirty dollars a gram yesterday! Why you tryina fuck me over?"

Darrel flashed his toothless grin and winked at Jenny. Mika thought it was funny how Jenny tried to talk ghetto when she was dealing with dealers, as if Darrel didn't know that she was some small town rich white girl.

"The price varies. The cops are watching all the hardware stores and pharmacies now. You buy too much Sudafed or muriatic acid and the feds will jump all over your ass. More risk. Higher price. I threw that half gram in there as a bonus. For anybody else, it's a hunnerd and a half a gram. I told you. This shit is hot right now."

"Damn! This is bullshit! You know how much I'm gonna have to sell this shit for to make my money back?"

"You can sell it for $40 a hit. Those shitkickers will still buy it. What else they gonna do? Get clean?" That seemed to tickle Darrel. He laughed loudly as he fell back onto the mattress.

The two Indian girls lying next to him could have been sisters, or perhaps even mother and daughter. They stared at Mika and Jenny, looking right through them as if they weren't even there. Their eyes reminded Mika of the water babies, soulless and empty.

"I won't make shit! I'll make, like, five dollars a hit even if I sell it for forty." Jenny was so angry she was turning red. The veins in her neck and forehead were sticking out as she jabbed her finger at Darrel like it was a weapon.

"Then you just sell smaller hits. Sell an eighth of a gram instead of a quarter. Tell those fuckin' shit kickers the same thing I'm tellin' you. The heat is on, so the price went up."

"At least give me five grams? Come on. A hundred a gram?"

Darrel looked her up and down, then turned his eyes toward Mika. Both Mika and Jenny's T-shirts were still translucent from the rain, and their breasts were clearly visible.

"I tell you what. You let me fuck you and your friend there, and I'll give you six grams for five."

Jenny shook her head and pulled Mika closer.

"Hell no! You so spun out you couldn't get it up anyway. Just sell me the shit so I can go."

"Oh, I can get it up. Believe me," Darrel replied, rubbing between his legs, stroking himself to an erection as he leered at the two young girls.

"Well, you're gonna have to stick to the tired-ass whores you got unless you want a statutory rape charge. We're both still in high school … and she's mine."

Jenny turned and kissed Mika on the lips. Darrel's eyes widened. His mouth dropped open in surprise, and he began to laugh, rolling around on the soiled mattress, holding his stomach as if he were afraid it would burst.

"Oh shit! You guys fuckin'? You two? You lick her pussy? Really?"

"Every chance I get," Mika said, stepping forward.

"So you don't like dick anymore?" Darrel Ray

asked Jenny.

"I still like dick, but I love pussy," Jenny said, licking her lips as she reached out and rubbed Mika's nearly bald head.

"Oh shit! Well, I guess that's worth another half a gram. Five grams for five hundred."

He handed Jenny five small ziplock bags filled with a whitish powder that Mika knew was meth. There wasn't a scale in sight, and Mika wondered how either of them knew how much drugs were in each bag, but she refrained from asking. She just wanted to get the hell out of there. Jenny pulled a wad of twenties as thick as her wrist out of her shorts and handed it to Darrel. Then she turned and walked out of the room, pulling Mika along with her.

"You take care, Darrel. I'll be back for more when this is gone."

"I know you will," Darrel answered. "My shit is the best. And if you get tired of chewing carpet, you can come see me." Darrel was still stroking himself through his dirty sweatpants.

"I won't be getting tired of this anytime soon."

Mika was surprised by Jenny's brazenness. They had only been lovers for less than an hour, but she didn't seem to have a single hesitation about telling the world that she was in love with another girl. Mika wasn't sure how she felt about that. This was still a small town, and people here weren't terribly open-minded about homosexuality, Indians least of all. But Mika had never given much of a fuck about what most of the rednecks in town thought. She didn't see why she should start giving a fuck now. Jenny was right. They were in love, so why should they hide it?

Darrel shouted at them as they walked back out the door. "Ya need to get that shit on video. You could sell it on the internet. Lesbian porn is real big right now, especially that barely legal shit. Fuck, I'll even film it for you!"

Mika and Jenny hurried out of the house and back across the half-dead garbage strewn lawn. Mika could hear the baby crying as they made it to the road. She had no doubt that the kid would be dead soon if Child Welfare didn't come get him first. She made a mental note to call them and report the baby's condition the first chance she got.

The two girls walked quickly down the road, trying to put as much distance as possible between them and Darrel Ray.

"Never take me to that shithole again. Darrel's a fucking pervert. Those drugs have fucked him up. I can't believe my brother was at a party there last night. I need to kick this shit if that's what it does to you."

"How far away is your dad's house?" Jenny asked.

"I think it's just a few blocks down the road."

CHAPTER 11

Joshua Rain's house looked like every other house on the rez except that it was better kept, with a manicured lawn and a vegetable garden. There was a 2009 black Dodge Ram Crew Cab in the driveway and a large Rottweiler chained to a tree in the front yard. The dog stared at Mika and Jenny as they walked up to the front door. It snarled but did not bark. Mika kept her eye on the big Rottweiler as she knocked on the door of her biological father's house.

Joshua was a big man. He was over six feet tall and well over two hundred pounds. His hair was cut short in a military crewcut with streaks of gray running through it. Even his eyebrows were salted with gray. His face was clean-shaven, and his smile was big and natural and contagious. It exploded across his face the minute he opened the door.

"Mika?"

"Yeah, it's me." Mika looked down at her feet, then behind her at Jenny. "This is my friend, Jenny. Jenny, this is … I don't know what to call you."

Joshua nodded. "Just call me Joshua."

"I need your help … Joshua just doesn't feel right. I feel like I should be calling you Dad. I mean, you are technically my father, right? If my mom had any guts, I would have grown up here with you on the reservation."

"Your mom was trying to do what was right by you. She was married, and life on the reservation is hard."

"She was taking the easy way out. She loved you. She told me. I think she still does."

Joshua nodded again and smiled tenderly, looking Mika up and down. He reached out and ruffled her short hair.

"See what happens when you come on the reservation by yourselves? You get scalped." When he laughed, it was full and rich. He rubbed his own buzzcut, still grinning wide. "You look like me now. Give me a hug."

He gathered Mika into his big, thick arms and

hugged her tight. Mika's body stiffened, and she didn't relax until he had released her.

"You have grown into a very beautiful young girl. You are always welcome here, Mika. It's been years since your mom brought you around. I didn't want to go see you because of your family. But you are *my* family. You're my only daughter, my only child."

Mika's eyes filled with tears. Even Jenny got misty eyed.

"So come on in. What made you come see me without your mom? How is she, by the way? I think you were six or seven the last time I saw either of you. How old are you now?"

"I'm almost seventeen."

"Wow. I can't believe it's been that long. And your mother? How is she?"

"Mom is good. She'd love to see you. You look good too, just like I remembered you. Just a little more gray. I came because I need your help, though. What do you know about water babies?"

Joshua's eyebrows raised, and his eyes widened, then narrowed in suspicion. He opened his mouth, quickly closed it, then opened it again. There was a look on his face that didn't seem natural. It seemed out of place on him. It was fear. And seeing it haunting Joshua's usually strong features unleashed the terror that had been slithering around inside Mika's stomach since she'd first seen the water babies crying in the Owens River.

"I guess you'd better have a seat. Do you want a drink?"

"Do you have any beer?" Jenny asked, and Mika gave her a disapproving look.

"Sure. Do you want one too?"

Mika was surprised. "Sure."

Mika looked over at Jenny, then grabbed her hand and pulled it into her lap, squeezing it in both of hers as Joshua walked into the kitchen. He came back carrying two 40 oz. bottles of Crazy Horse. Mika saw him look quizzically at Jenny's hand in her lap, but she didn't care. She had already decided not to hide who she was, and she wasn't going to go back on that so soon. Joshua nodded as if a question had been asked and answered, then handed them both their beers.

"Thank you," Mika said as she cracked open the forty.

Joshua turned and walked back into the kitchen. He came back with a shot glass and a bottle of Wild Turkey. He poured himself a shot, then sat down on a big tan suede Lazy Boy across from Mika and

Jenny.

"I need a little something stronger for this. Why do you want to know about water babies?"

"Because I've seen them."

Joshua chuckled and shook his head. He poured himself another shot. "If you'd seen them, you'd be dead."

Mika looked at Jenny. That was certainly not the response she'd been expecting. "Well, I'm not. But everyone around me seems to be dying."

Joshua scooted forward in his chair. "And what did they look like?"

"They had really pale skin, like there was no blood in their bodies, like vampires. Like they had never been out of the water. They had black hair and black eyes with big round pupils. And they never blinked. That was the first thing I noticed. Their eyes never blinked. Their mouths were big too, like a fish. And I got the impression that they had too many teeth. I don't know how many teeth a baby is supposed to have, but this looked like it would have been too many teeth even for an adult. And they were making these crying sounds. They looked like they were drowning in the river, but it was like they weren't crying hard enough. It's hard to explain, but they weren't screaming the way a normal baby would if it was drowning. There was no panic in their voices. This was like the way a baby would cry if they had stubbed their toe ten minutes before, like they were crying over something that had happened a long time ago rather than over what was happening to them now.

"And then I saw my uncle in the water the next day. He was in the stream. He came from under the water, but that's impossible because the stream is barely deep enough to cover your ankles in most spots, but he was completely underwater. He just floated straight up out of it until it was like he was standing on the water."

"And what did he look like? Did he look normal?"

"Well, he was naked and he was all beaten up the way he looked the last time I saw him." Mika didn't want to tell Joshua why her uncle had been beaten up when she'd seen him last. She was still ashamed about what that sick bastard had done to her.

Joshua ran his hand over his face and looked down at the floor. It was obvious that he believed her and that it worried him, but more than that, it terrified him. Mika was relieved that there was now an adult who believed her but even more scared than before because that meant there was a chance she wasn't crazy, that she wasn't hallucinating, and her friends were really being murdered by little cherubic demons that lived in the water. It meant she might be next.

"Have you seen them too?" Joshua asked Jenny.

"I haven't, but I was there when Mika saw her Uncle Jeff. It was just so dark. I didn't see anything."

Joshua nodded. "If you really have seen them and they didn't kill you, there has to be a reason. There has to be some reason why they would let you live."

"Like what?" Mika asked.

Joshua shrugged. "Maybe they had pity on you or maybe they felt some kinship with you."

"Kinship?"

"You are like them … a half-breed, a pariah. Not accepted by the Paiutes. Not welcome anywhere."

Mika felt wounded. Did he mean that he didn't accept her either?

"So they're real? They exist? I'm not just crazy?"

"You are a Christian, right? Are angels and demons real?"

"I think they are. I don't know."

"Well, I think the Pahoha, the water babies, are real. Probably for the same reasons you think angels are real. My mother and grandmother used to tell me stories about them when I was a kid. She used to make me carry a small bag of pine nuts with me whenever I went to the creek to swim. I would have to throw the pine nuts into the water as an offering to the Pahoha, to appease them so they would leave me alone. Whenever someone would drown in the river or the creek, she would tell me that the water babies had gotten them. Sometimes, kids would just disappear. They wouldn't even find their bodies. We always believed that it was the Pahoha who had taken them."

"What are they?"

Joshua knocked back his shot, then placed the glass and the bottle on the floor. He rubbed his face with his hand again, then looked at Mika for a long moment before speaking. Mika felt a sense of dread creep over her. She wasn't sure she wanted to hear this. She took a deep breath and let it out slow. She squeezed Jenny's hand and rubbed her arm for comfort.

"The Pahoha are the children of the Lady of the Water and her Paiute lover. They say that they were both cast out by the tribe centuries ago and their vengeful offspring have haunted us ever since."

"Are they ghosts or demons?"

"They are both and neither. The elders say that in olden times, when the Paiutes were camped on the western side by Yosemite, a young hunter returned from the hunt with a beautiful young woman. The woman had ghostly pale skin and long black hair like the feathers of a raven. He told the tribe that she had appeared to him out of the water, and he proclaimed his love for her. The tribespeople didn't trust her. They feared her. She had eyes as black as a moonless night, and there was something evil in them. But they accepted her because of the young Paiute's obvious love for her.

"The next morning, the tribe awoke to find that water had surrounded their camp as they slept. They moved their camp, but wherever they went, the water would be there when they awoke, creeping closer and closer. The tribespeople begged the young Paiute to leave her. They were terrified of her and believed that she intended to drown them all. But the young hunter would not abandon the woman he loved. Then the chief of the tribe banished them from their camp, fearing that they would all be drowned by the water that she brought in her dreams.

"The couple moved outside the camp, and when his relatives visited him, they noticed the woman would not leave the water. The young Paiute looked sickly and pale from spending so much time in the water. He eventually died, but not before he had fathered many children with the mysterious woman. The tribe called their children Pahoha, water babies, because they never left the water. The children were not accepted either. Grieving for her dead husband and enraged because the tribe would not accept her children as their own, the Lady of the Water cast a spell over her babies and then drowned them all.

"Now the Pahoha can be heard weeping like babies at night, and anyone who sees them are drawn into the water and drowned. My mother used to say that she sometimes saw their tiny footprints in the mud after a rain storm."

"But how are they able to look like my Uncle Jeff?"

"The legends say Pahoha are mischievous shapeshifters that can sense your deepest fears and desires and mimic them. They can become your nightmares and your fantasies. They say they assume the shape of your loved ones in order to lure you into the water. But even if they don't drown you, even if you escape, just seeing them brings bad luck. My mother would tell me that once you have seen them, you are forever cursed and it won't be long before …" Joshua caught himself too late.

"Before you die? They say that anyone who sees them dies, right? That means that I'm going to die too, right?" Mika tilted up her beer and drained it dry. "Do you have a cigarette? I need a smoke."

Joshua reached into his pocket and handed her a pack of Marlboros. She shook one out and placed it between her lips. Joshua struck a match on his jeans and lit it for her. She blew the smoke out slowly, her bottom lip trembling and tears spilling down her cheeks.

"I don't want to die. Drowning is probably the worst thing I can imagine besides burning alive. I don't want to die that way."

Joshua stood up and sat next to Mika, between her and Jenny. He wrapped his arms around her, and Mika tensed. Joshua was her real father. It was his seed that gave her life. But she barely knew him, and after what her uncle had done to her, any affection shown to her by older men made her uncomfortable. Mika stood and walked to the other end of the couch. She gestured for Jenny to scoot over, then sat with Jenny now squeezed between her and Joshua.

"It's just a legend. Nothing is absolute. It could all be bullshit."

"But you don't think so, do you? You think it's real?"

"They haven't killed you yet. They say that you can make friends with them. Some Shamans are said to be able to communicate with them and use them to perform good. Maybe they have befriended you. Maybe that's why they haven't killed you."

"Then why are they killing all my friends?"

"Are you sure that it's your friends they are killing? Maybe they are protecting you. Maybe they are trying to isolate you, to make you come to them so you can become like them."

Mika's eyebrows furrowed. "Isolate me?"

"If you have no one else to turn to, maybe they think you will come to them, or like I said, maybe they just think they are protecting you."

Mika sat in silence. It was Jenny who spoke up.

"So how do we stop them? How do we kill them?"

Joshua shook his head solemnly. "You can't kill them. They aren't alive."

Jenny draped a protective arm around Mika. Her face was stern and serious. There was a determination in her eyes to protect the woman she loved. Mika was touched, but it didn't make her feel any safer. All she could feel was her own slowly creeping terror spreading through her like an infection. A fatal sense of doom settled over her. She didn't think she could beat this thing. She had never felt in control of anything in her life. Things always happened to her while she just sat helplessly, trying to make it through, usually with the help of some drug or other. She not only feared for her own life but the lives of everyone around her, everyone she loved.

"Then how do we stop them?"

"You have to appease them, make friends with them. You have to give them an offering."

"Like pine nuts?" Jenny asked.

"If they have latched on to her like she says they have, then it's probably going to take more than pine nuts."

"Will you help us? I love Mika. I don't want to see her die."

There was a loud screech, and they all turned around. An owl sat on the windowsill with a field mouse in its beak. The owl was as white as snow. The girls relaxed, but Joshua looked even more terrified than ever. His hand went to his throat as if checking for a pulse. His eyes remained fixed on the owl until it finally flew away.

"I'll do all I can. I don't want to see either of you die."

CHAPTER 12

Tonya Bowhunter was leaning against a car down the street from Joshua Rain's house with three other girls from the reservation. They were huddled together under a thick stand of trees trying to stay dry as they passed a forty of Crazy Horse back and forth, alternating between that and a big fat cigar filled with marijuana and PCP.

Mika stepped out onto the porch and hugged her father goodbye. She failed to notice the large Indian girls, but they noticed her. Mika was too intent on her father and trying to figure out how to stop the water babies. The last thing on her mind was being jumped by a gang of fat reservation hoes.

"Don't worry. I'll help you figure this out. It will be okay."

Mika kissed her father's cheek. "Thank you."

Jenny hugged Joshua as well, and then the two girls began walking back down Pa Ha Lane. Jenny had her arm around Mika's shoulder, and Mika had both arms wrapped around Jenny's waist, with her head resting on her shoulder.

"I don't know what we're going to do. How the fuck are we supposed to appease these things?"

"Maybe we can just stay away from the river?"

"And the creek? And the stream? You heard Joshua … uh … my dad. These things can be anywhere. In any lake, any river, any pond. Besides, he said that just seeing them was bad luck. It could be my fault that everyone's dying."

"It's not your fault. These things are evil or something."

"But what if it isn't real? What if there's no such thing as water babies and it's just my schizophrenia making me hallucinate, and Howard just got drunk and drowned himself by accident, and Teddy just fell asleep behind the wheel with the car running because of all the drugs he took that night, and Johnny was just drinking too much when he drove off the bridge? What if none of it had anything to do with little demons or ghosts or whatever they are and they're all just coincidences? What if this is just some old bullshit legend?"

"I didn't want to say anything, but I can't help wondering the same thing. You've been doing a shitload of meth, and you haven't taken your medication in weeks. You've been pretty fucked up lately, and it's not like people don't get high or drunk and kill themselves all the time around here."

Mika rubbed her fists against her temples. "But it all feels so real! It just makes sense in some fucked up way. I had never even heard of water babies. I didn't know shit about any old Indian legends when I saw them. Why would I be hallucinating about things I didn't even know existed?"

"I don't know, Mika, but I'm scared too. That shit your dad was saying about being cursed just by seeing them. That shit really freaked me out. I don't want you to die. We should just leave town now. Get far away from here. We could move to Las Vegas or LA, where there's no such thing as water demons and curses and shit."

"That would be nice. I bet there's a lot more girls like us in the city. You know ... lesbians."

Jenny laughed and kissed Mika on the forehead. "Damn. It sounds dirty the way you say it. I guess this thing still freaks you out, huh? I mean, this thing between us? Is it going too fast? I mean, one minute we're fucking in the woods, and the next we're going to see your biological father. It's too fast, huh?"

Mika smiled bashfully and turned away. "It is a little fast, but I like it. I mean, it feels right. I just need a little time to get used to it is all. I mean, you were my best friend just this morning, and now you're my lover. I'm just tryin' to get used to it."

"I'm sorry. I know you haven't had that long to think about it, but I've been thinking about it for months. I really do love you."

"I love you too, Jenny. You've always been my best friend. I'm just sayin', this is a small town and people aren't real open-minded. We're going to catch a lot of shit from people."

"I won't let anything happen to you."

Mika hugged Jenny tighter, then tilted her head up to kiss her. That's when she finally spotted Tonya Bowhunter.

"What the fuck are you two nasty bitches doin' here?"

Tonya stood up and began walking toward them, splashing through puddles of rain in big basketball sneakers the size of construction boots. She looked enormous. She was taller than Jenny and about twenty or thirty pounds heavier, And the three other girls with her were nearly identical in size. Her hair was thick and frizzy, puffed out like an afro, as if she had blown it dry but forgotten to do anything else with it. The rain quickly smashed her big frizzy hair flat as she stepped out from under the trees and into the full force of the downpour. She was wearing a wife-beater with long blue basketball shorts that came down to her knees. She looked genuinely angry, as if Mika and Jenny had done her some unforgivable wrong just by walking down her street.

"We came to see my dad."

"Joshua ain't your fuckin' dad, white girl. Just cause he donated some sperm to your mom, that don't make you a Paiute. Don't ever think you're one of us."

"Leave her the fuck alone, Tonya. We ain't tryin' to fuck with you. We're just tryin' to get home."

"You stay the fuck out of this shit, you fuckin' dyke! You'll fuck anything, won't you? Our men, other bitches. You naaaasty fuckin' slut!"

"Fuck you, you fat bitch! You're just mad 'cause don't nobody want none of your fat-ass pussy!"

The first punch sounded to Mika as if a gun had gone off. The wet smack and crunch of Tonya's knuckles colliding with Jenny's nose made Mika's stomach flip. It was the most sickening sound she could have imagined. Jenny's nose crushed beneath the impact, spraying blood across her face and dropping her to her knees. Mika was still holding on to her when she fell, and Mika went down as well, landing on her back. The back of her head hit the concrete, and Mika nearly blacked out.

The big Indian girl raised her foot and kicked Jenny in the face. Jenny's jaw unhinged and hung at an odd angle, drooling blood from the corner of her mouth. The expression on Tonya's face was one of mindless rage. There seemed to be no intelligence behind her eyes, like the eyes of some rabid, feral dog. Mika had heard that Tonya and her crew smoked weed laced with angel dust. She was obviously whacked on something. All reason had abandoned her. She looked completely insane.

"What did you say to me, bitch? What the fuck did you say to me?"

Jenny toppled onto her back, and blood poured from her nose like rainwater. Her eyes rolled up into her skull.

"Stop! Stop! Get away from her! She's hurt!"

One of the other girls kicked Mika in the head, and Mika rolled over and covered her face and head to avoid further blows. She screamed as Tonya launched another kick at Jenny's face that sent blood splattering onto the road in thick red dollops.

"Stop it! Stop hurting her!"

"Bitch, shut the fuck up!" One of the other girls kicked Mika in her ribs, exploding the wind from her lungs.

Mika moaned and rolled onto her back, curling her knees to her chest and holding her bruised ribs with both arms. Tonya was now sitting on top of Jenny's chest. She had her fingers snarled in the girl's hair and was banging Jenny's skull into the asphalt. There was a sticky wet crack every time her head smacked into the blacktop. The back of Jenny's cranium was dripping red. Her hair was completely drenched with blood.

"You fuckin' white whore! You nasty dyke bitch! Fuck you! Fuck yoooooou!"

Jenny's skull had begun to lose its shape. The back of it had completely caved in, and Mika could see her friend's brain peeking through the cracks in her skull. Jenny's arms and legs were trembling and convulsing, and Mika thought for a moment how closely her death throes resembled the throes of ecstasy. Mika was looking in Jenny's eyes just as the light in them went out forever, as if someone had blown out a candle—one minute her friend and lover, and the next an empty shell of lifeless meat.

"Nooooooo! Nooohohoooo! No. No. No!"

"Oh fuck, you killed her! That bitch is dead! Let's get the fuck out of here!"

The girls ran off, leaving Tonya alone with Mika, with Jenny's corpse twitching in the street at her feet. Mika crawled over to her friend and cradled her head in her lap. Blood poured from Jenny's ears and nose, as well as from her ruptured misshapen skull.

Tonya knelt down onto one knee, scowling murderously at Mika. "You'd better not say nothin', bitch, or I'll kill you too. I didn't mean to hurt her. She shouldn't have fucked with me. She shouldn't have pissed me off."

Then, bizarrely, the big Indian girl placed a hand on Mika's shoulder, almost tenderly. Her face softened, and her voice lowered to a whisper. "I'm sorry. Really, I'm sorry. I know you loved her. I could tell. I'm sorry. You two were always really tight." And then she ran off down the street after her friends.

Mika stared down at Jenny's blood-smeared

face. She brushed the hair from her cheeks and forehead. Some of Jenny's teeth were missing. Her face was badly bruised, almost unrecognizable, and her nose had been pulverized. Mika had experienced true love for the first time in her life, had found her soulmate, only to watch her get brutally murdered all in the same day.

She had no doubt now that she had been cursed. The Pahoha had cursed her. Jenny would still be alive if Mika had just jumped into the Owens River and drowned when she was supposed to. She hugged Jenny's battered skull to her chest and stroked her fingers through her dead lover's blood-soaked hair.

"Your hair looked so pretty today. I forgot to tell you that. You looked so beautiful."

When the tears came, they completely overwhelmed her. She screamed her throat raw as lightning ripped through the sky and the rain began to pour harder. Doors opened up and down the block, and people walked tentatively from their homes, moving slowly toward her, too late to help her, too late to save Jenny.

Blood leaked from Jenny's mouth, dripping onto Mika's leg and into her lap.

"I love you, Jenny. You're my best friend."

Mika closed Jenny's eyes slowly, then kissed her softly. The rain washed the tears from Mika's cheeks down onto Jenny's face, diluting the blood and washing it into the sewer. The coppery taste of blood coated Mika's lips. Mika continued to weep as adults from the reservation surrounded her. She heard someone call for an ambulance. Someone else called for the police. Mika kissed Jenny once more.

"Goodbye, Jenny. I will see you soon."

Mika stood and began walking down the street. Joshua stood in her way, and Mika walked slowly around him without acknowledging his presence. There was something Cliff had said to her that was bothering her, something about seeing Uncle Jeff by the creek last night. But it couldn't have been her uncle. He had moved to Texas after her dad had tried to beat him to death. But Cliff had seen him too, by the stream. Only it hadn't been Uncle Jeff. It was the water babies, the Pahoha. They had plucked the image of Uncle Jeff from her mind and tried to use it to lure her into the water. Cliff must have seen the water babies too, and that meant he was in danger as well.

"Mika? What happened? Are you okay? Come inside. Are you bleeding? Mika?" Joshua grabbed her by the shoulders and tried to steer her toward his house.

Mika screamed when he touched her and jerked free of his grasp. She ran. She ran between houses, across fields, and down a long dirt road that led directly to the creek. The rain came down even harder. Mika found herself splashing through deep puddles. Her shoes sank into the mud as she raced down the unpaved road, leaving the houses behind. She could hear the sound of running water. The faster and further she ran, the louder the sound grew.

The rain fell without relent, increasing in intensity and drenching the earth. Lightning struck the ground somewhere nearby, followed by an almost deafening clap of thunder and the smell of sulfur and ozone. The sound of running water was soon joined by another sound, a sound Mika had come to recognize far too well ... the sound of babies crying. Mika slowed to a fast walk until she reached the edge of the creek.

As she had expected, the Pahoha were there. Almost a dozen of them, floating in the torrential waters, some weeping, some giggling humorlessly, some eerily silent. They turned to face Mika as she approached. They stopped weeping, stopped giggling, and began swimming slowly toward her, their frigid, unblinking black eyes fixed on her. Mika balled her hands into fists and yelled.

"Leave my friends alone! Don't hurt anyone else. Just take me. Take me!"

There was a fierce current flowing through the creek, eroding the earth on either side of the water. The heavy rainfall dotted the water, creating ripples that were quickly dispersed by the roiling tide. Mika was not surprised when a large figure emerged from the waves, rising slowly from the bottom of the creek. He had the same bruised and blackened eyes and busted lip and nose he'd had the last time she'd seen him.

"Fuckin' Uncle Jeff. Why you? Why the fuck does it always have to be you? I fucking hate you!"

"I'm not just a memory, little muffin. They didn't just pluck me from your mind. I came from down here, in the water, where your dad put me the day he murdered me. The day you told him I touched you."

Mika's jaw dropped. She shook her head slowly. "My dad? No. No. He didn't kill you. I saw you leave after the fight."

"I came back that night to talk to him. I wanted to explain myself. He beat me with Cliff's baseball bat. Knocked me unconscious. Then he drove me to the river and put my body in a bag filled with rocks. I was still alive when he threw me in."

"No. He wouldn't do that. He wouldn't."

But it made sense. That's why he didn't call the cops. That's why he refused to talk about it, why he wanted her to just forget the whole thing. He had killed his own brother to protect her. He had cared after all.

The other water babies began to slowly transform, metamorphosizing, growing. Their flesh stretched and muscles hypertrophied, bones popping and snapping, elongating, reorganizing beneath their skin. Mika began to recognize the new faces slowly forming like clay sculpted by invisible hands. Howard, Teddy, Johnny, then Cliff, and, finally, Jenny.

"We're all down here. We're waiting for you."

"Jenny? Cliff?"

"I came down to the creek to find Uncle Jeff. I wanted to make things right. I wanted to punish him for hurting you. But they pulled me in."

Mika dropped to her knees by the edge of the creek. Jenny was dead, and now so was her little brother. She had lost everything. She thought about what Joshua had said about the Pahoha trying to isolate her so that she would give up all hope and come to them. She was almost there. She had no one left now.

"Oh, Cliff. I'm sorry. I'm so sorry. You didn't have to do this. This is all my fault."

A loud screech pierced through the sound of the rain, and Mika knew before she even looked up that it was the owl again. The same ivory bird of prey she'd seen outside Joshua's window before Jenny was murdered. It now sat on a branch that hung down over the creek. It was staring at her as if waiting to see what she would do next. Mika lowered her head and continued to weep for her dead brother.

When she looked up again, her dead friends were standing at the water's edge with the waves lapping at their legs, waiting. Mika looked directly into Jenny's eyes. "Was this my fault too? Did you all die because of me?"

"Come with us. Come stay with us, Mika. We love you."

Jenny reached out for her. "I love you, Mika. Come with me."

Mika stood. Rain poured down her face. Her body hitched and jerked as she sobbed. Her heart felt as if it had ruptured in her chest. "I love you too, Jenny. I love you so much."

Mika removed her muddy Converses. She peeled off her bloody shorts and T-shirt. The water babies slowly morphed back into the little black-eyed amphibians they were, bodies melting and reshaping like candle-wax sculptures. All except for Jenny, who remained standing in the water with her arms held out, beseeching Mika to join her. She looked so beautiful.

Her hair was long and blonde and flowing, just as it had been this morning. She was naked, and her breasts and hips looked full and ripe, nipples erect. Her lips were parted slightly, and her eyes looked sad and needy, hungry. Mika wanted her so badly. She needed her.

One of the water babies sat squatting on a stone like a frog in the middle of the creek. It was smiling at her with teeth that looked too plentiful, too big, too sharp. Mika ignored it and turned her attention back to Jenny. She took the first step into the creek. The water lapped violently at her heels, almost sweeping her off balance. She took another step. Jenny floated backward on the waves, arms still outstretched, beckoning to Mika, urging her to follow her further into the water.

Mika waded out until the water was up to

her throat. The babies swam toward her. Jenny gathered her into her arms, pulling Mika into her frigid embrace and wrapping her legs around Mika's waist. Mika kissed her deeply as they both sank beneath the waves. The babies rushed in to join them, latching onto the couple one by one until Mika found herself smothered by a dozen grinning white babies. Her lungs filled with water, and Mika began to panic, all of her survival instincts awakened as her brain began to starve for oxygen. She struggled to free herself, fighting for air, but Jenny and the babies held her tight. The surface of the water was mere inches from the top of her head, but she might as well have been fathoms deep.

She ceased struggling, slowly losing consciousness. The Pahoha that had taken the shape of Jenny reverted back to its original form, and Mika found herself staring into two cold obsidian eyes. She screamed with the last of her breath. Above her, the dark, tumultuous clouds drifted apart and the sun broke through, revealing a beautiful blue sky.

She saw Joshua at the edge of the creek, looking for her, hands cupped around his mouth, calling her name. She wondered what she would look like when she came for him—or rather, when the water babies did, wearing her face. She wondered if her other father, the man who had raised her, would come looking for her. If he would wade down into the creek to save her when he saw her drowning, beer in one hand, Camel cigarette in the other, cursing and angry. If her hair would still be short and choppy when he saw her, if she would still have bleeding scratches on her arms and chest, or if they would at least make her beautiful again.

All she had ever wanted was for her father to think she was beautiful, for him to love her and accept her. She had waited so long for him to show her that he cared. Now she would wait for him just a little while longer. She would wait for him beneath the water with her new friends.

WRATH JAMES WHITE is a former World Class Heavyweight Kickboxer, a professional Kickboxing and Mixed Martial Arts trainer, distance runner, performance artist, and former street brawler, who is now known for creating some of the most disturbing works of fiction in print.

Wrath is the author of such extreme horror classics as THE RESURRECTIONIST (now a major motion picture titled "Come Back To Me") SUCCULENT PREY, and it's sequel PREY DRIVE, YACCUB'S CURSE, 400 DAYS OF OPPRESSION, SACRIFICE, VORACIOUS, TO THE DEATH, THE REAPER, SKINZZ, EVERYONE DIES FAMOUS IN A SMALL TOWN, THE BOOK OF A THOUSAND SINS, HIS PAIN, POPULATION ZERO, IF YOU DIED TOMORROW I WOULD EAT YOUR CORPSE, HARDCORE KELLI, and many others. He is the co-author of TERATOLOGIST co-written with the king of extreme horror, Edward Lee, SOMETHING TERRIBLE co-written with his son Sultan Z. White, ORGY OF SOULS co-written with Maurice Broaddus, HERO and THE KILLINGS both co-written with J.F. Gonzalez, POISONING EROS co-written with Monica J. O'Rourke, MASTER OF PAIN co-written with Kristopher Rufty, and BOY'S NIGHT co-written with Matt Shaw among others.

Wrath lives and works in Austin, TX.